Renato Belindro

MONASTERY

Season 1

Episode 8

Love Child

Copyright © 2024 Renato Belindro

All rights reserved

The characters and events portrayed in this book are fictitious. Any similarity to real persons, living or dead, is coincidental and not intended by the author.

No part of this book may be reproduced, or stored in a retrieval system, or transmitted in any form or by any means, be they electronic, mechanical, photocopying, recording, or otherwise, without express written permission of the publisher.

Edited by Renato Belindro
Cover design by Ellen Harrison

*Para o meu tio Miguel.
Desculpa lá qualquer coisinha.*

Previously, on Monastery

Let's do a recap of the investigation so far, shall we? After all, so much has been uncovered. From surprise correspondence...

Thomas gets up and smiles, delighted to see a record player live and in color.

When he picks up the record, a sheet of paper almost comes along with it.

"What's that?" Henry asks.

"A letter from Grandpa."

Thomas takes out the new poem they received and puts it side-by-side with the code.

"Look at the numbers. 7-7-0-4-0-9. Seven winds, the seven of us, zero chance, four children, zero tolerance, nine yards."

"Holy crap!" "What the hell?" "I don't get it."

"I take back what I said before. These poems we have been getting are not arbitrary," Thomas says, "the person sending them knows something, something big."

David's hand goes limp, and Thomas catches the letter mid-air. "'If you wanna see your dog alive again, you better drop this whole thing. Otherwise, you'll get him back in installments. Signed, Albert.'"

He looks up at his Godfather and sees that all expression has gone from his face. David's lips tremble before he can finally mutter, "R-Rocky?"

To confidential information...

Thomas' eyes reach an unprecedented diameter when the reporter slides her claw-like nail down his own father's chest, then tracing it around Walt's badge.
"Cora?" my son-in-law says.
"Yeah?"
"If I didn't want you when you were young and sort of attractive, why would I want you now?"
"Then tell *you* what: give me everything you have on that grave-digging perv, or I leak the report I made when your father-in-law died, that I didn't put out at the time."
Walt almost loses grip of the bottle. While Thomas' every sense perks up.

"So, just to make sure I understand," Nicole says, "this ripped piece of paper is a DNA test your uncle Francis took, and the unnamed second person referred to is his mother."
"Yes."
"Any chance the woman in question might actually be Cassandra?"
David shrugs his shoulders. "Why'd he get a DNA test to prove his mother is his mother?"
"Fair enough. Another thing: you just took this from your uncle's room?"

"Yeah?"
"And you don't think he's gonna notice it's missing?"

To enough trinkets to fill up a horror movie nursery.

Thomas furrows his brow. He then runs to the crib and grabs the railing. "This. Henry was weird after touching it."
Thomas squats, sliding his hands around the rails of the crib, as he takes a closer look at one of the corners where the bar meets the railing, close to the screw.
"Is – is that blood?"

Fred walks away and Thomas reaches behind the fridge. Instead of the spoon, he takes out a toy car.
"Really? Henry!"
"What?"
"One of your toys was behind the fridge."
All Henry can do is shake his head and walk away.
Thomas furrows his brows. He picks up the spoon and puts it down on the table with the car. It's metallic blue, and the rare variation with imprinted flames on the doors.
Rarer still for the blood covering its hood.
All the scattered pieces of the puzzle dance around my grandson's head, mocking him for his inability to put them together. The toy car. The crib. The chest and the key, the number code, George

Turner. What could they all mean? How do they fit together?

Do they even?

I think it's time we started getting some answers. Don't you?

***

Teaser

Everyone's got their share of places they hate going to. Most will agree they hate funerals – not even up for discussion – while many will say they can't stand hospitals or being on an airplane. Let's not even get into the college students who must be terrified of their classes, since they never set foot in there.

Of all the above, the hospital is the only one I frequented on a semi-regular basis – when you've had as many kids as I have, you get to know it like the back of your hand. Cassandra, however, was always a patient, never a visitor, which not only resulted in her disdain for the place, but also for a lack of awareness of where each corridor winds up. Making it very fun for me to go back in time and see her trying to find her way through the wings of the Portalegrum hospital, like Theseus lost in the labyrinth. Well, it's perhaps more reasonable to compare my widow to the minotaur.

The year was 1997, though not for long, and Cassandra tried to hide her affliction as she paced down the halls, cradling her pregnant belly in her hands. She was never one to ask for help – unless she needed money – so she wasn't about to admit to any of the personnel just how lost she was. Not that she needed to.

"Should I get you a map, dear?"

Cassandra closed her eyes and tried to count to ten, but only made it halfway through. When she turned around, with a look that would scare the bejesus out of both Theseus *and* the minotaur, she came face-to-face with the head nurse of the hospital: my dear sister, Doris.

"This is the coma ward," Doris said, "you have to go down one story and go straight ahead, room 108. Stairs are to your right."

My wife turned around without so much as a 'thank you.'

"Cassandra?"

What now?

"I must say, I was absolutely flabbergasted. Such a tragedy, bless her. So shortly after she was told of the pregnancy, no less. I wonder how the father of the child is feeling now."

My wife didn't have to turn around to see the derisive smirk on her sister-in-law's face – she could *feel* it. Doris knew. She had to know.

That stupid cow always knew everything.

"Well, thank God everything turned out alright," Doris continued. "They're both fine, she'll be released soon. And I should get back to work."

That she did; both of them parted ways without any goodbyes. When my wife finally made it to room 108, she pulled the curtain back with such force that it nearly came flying off, making the patient she was seeing jump in her bed.

"W-What are you doing here?"

Celeste's chin trembled so that it was hard to get the words out. Talking to Cassandra was difficult

14

enough under normal circumstances, but there? Like that? Mission impossible.

"I'm your emergency contact," my wife said, putting down her purse on the bedside table.

Celeste froze in place. The whole experience up to that point had been horrifying, and she feared it was about to get worse.

"How are you?" Cassandra asked.

"I-I'm fine," Celeste said, moving her hands down her belly, even more salient than her neighbor's, as if trying to hide it. "E-Everything's fine."

Cassandra moved closer to the bed. "I was so scared, you have no idea. When they called me, I dropped everything and got here as fast as I could."

Celeste was touched, though deeply confused. Why wasn't she bringing up the –

"You should have told me what you were going through," Cassandra said, "I'm hurt you didn't."

There it was. The tears came out of Celeste like someone had opened a flood gate. "I-I'm sorry."

Cassandra put her hand over her neighbor's. "It's okay." Celeste sobbed as my wife reached out to feel the gauze on her forehead. "Any stitches?"

"F-Fourteen."

"So many. Still, you were lucky, weren't you?"

Celeste nodded, which made the tears slide down her neck and dampen her hospital gown. "I couldn't believe it w-when they told me. I thought – oh, God, Cassandra, I wanted to end this, I was going to, b-but I couldn't and... Right after I fell, I-I thought I was going to die, and, and then – I thought I was going to lose him, I –"

Cassandra shushed her and stroked her hair, much blonder then than it is now. "You didn't. You didn't."

"I-I guess God had a different plan."

My wife smiled. "How long are they keeping you?"

"O-Overnight. Just to make sure."

"Good. I'll swing by in the morning, take you home."

Celeste couldn't believe her ears. Who was this Cassandra?

"I'll come by your place every day, till you're up on your feet again." She caressed her friend's cheek. "I promise."

Celeste got so teary-eyed she couldn't even see her neighbor anymore. Cassandra was nothing but a wet blur.

A blur that grew clearer as she inched closer to Celeste's face, looked her in the eyes and said, almost in a whisper, "Then I'm going to destroy you, Celeste. I'm going to take back everything you thought you could steal from me, and then some. Till you're nothing but a hollow reminder of the worthless whore you once were."

The words came over Celeste like a tidal wave. When Cassandra kissed her forehead, she knew her fate was sealed.

"I don't know about God's plan," my wife said as she stood up, "but what I have in store for you will make you wish you'd died on that fall."

She grabbed her purse again and walked out, holding her stomach in her hands. Leaving in her trail a sobbing, weeping, broken shell.

In that oh-so-dramatic moment, my son Francis gave his first kick.

Celeste didn't even notice.

***

Narrator
Albert Keane

Starring
David Childs
Thomas Ford
Fred Scott
Henry Keane
Nicole Carter
Francis Keane
Maggie Childs
Beth St. Esprit
Rick Stevens
Madam Witch
with
Cassandra Keane
and
Rocky Childs

Guest Starring
Glory Gardner
Charlie Keane
Alfie Leeds   Martin Ford
Walt Ford   Tony Childs
Mutt Stevens   Cora Leeds
with
Celeste Colm

Special Guest Star
Doris Plum

Act 1

Elizabeth St. Esprit was born on April 2nd, 1929. Now, for those us who didn't skip math, that adds up to nine whole decades of a life well lived, where nearly every joy you could dream up was felt at its most intense: from a forbidden love affair that blossomed into an airtight marriage, to the spoils of her husband's successful business, not to mention her own success in helping so many expectant mothers bring their children into the world.

The grievances balanced out the delights, of course. Both of Nana's own pregnancies were stillborn. Her brother was lost to the Second War, her parents to cancer. In fact, in her lifespan, Nana Beth buried almost as many people as she delivered. In my case, she was there for both. Yet her faith powered her through all the hardships, helping her to find the silver lining each time. But, as she lies still and helpless on her nephew's bed, forced to stare at the empty blue wall in front of her, she can't help but wonder where the good in this can be found.

"Nana?" a little voice says at the door. "What would you like for breakfast? Eggs, toast?"

A faint smile forms on her aged lips. There's the answer right there. 'Good' sleeps in the bed across from hers.

"Whatever's easier, Henry," she says, "I'm so sorry to trouble you."

Still in his summer PJ's, Henry adjusts the sheet over her body. "It's okay, I always make breakfast for everyone. At least you have an excuse why you need me to do it, the others don't."

Nana chuckles. "But it's still one more mouth to feed."

"Fred's not here. If you can take his bed, you can have his breakfast too." Henry moves to the window. "Are you hot? Want me to close this?"

"No, dear, I'm fine. Just turn my head to the right if you can. So I can see the movement in the hall."

He obliges, pushing her head gently over the pillow. "I asked Grandma if we could bring the TV in here from the kitchen, but she says it broke."

Yeah, that's what happens when someone shoots at it.

"That's alright, dear."

Henry heads for the door, after making sure Nana's positioned comfortably.

"Henry?"

He turns back.

"Don't ever lose that, honey."

Henry looks confused. "What?"

"Life's going to be hard. It's going to keep throwing everything it can at you. I think this summer is already teaching you that."

Henry puts his hands in the pockets of his PJ shorts, not knowing what to say.

"Life's gonna try to make you mean. Make you jaded. You can't let it, it's not worth it. Keep doing the good you do."

Henry smiles. "If I'm good – like you, Nana – will I get to live for as long as you have?"

She smiles back at him. "If you're good, sweetheart – truly good – then you'll get to live forever."

Nana has no way of knowing this, but at this moment, Henry makes a vow to her, and to himself, in his little heart. A vow he will never break.

And Henry has no way of knowing just how right Nana is.

*

"Breaking news in the George Turner murder case – police have found what appears to be the weapon used to take the life of Monastery's longstanding mortician. Details are being uncovered as we –"

Doesn't take long for Cora's words to peter out in my wife's ears. They're replaced by an overpowering anxiety, if the waves pulsating inside her brain are any indication.

"That can't be good."

Cassandra jumps, literally. She had no idea Francis was standing behind her the entire time.

"You told me you got rid of the trophy!" she tells him, in as low a tone as she can muster.

"I did, I buried it."

"Where?"

"Next to the soccer field."

Cassandra doesn't know whether to slap her forehead or his. "You hid a murder weapon in a place visited by fifty drunks every weekend?"

"You said to do it away from Devil's Creek. I thought that was far enough!"

For the love of God, kid, it was a cheap copper trophy, you couldn't have melted it in the fireplace? Amateurs!

Cassandra leans against the back of the couch, between two of the holes Francis punched in with my gun. I forgot to mention they're in the living room. You can get caught up in the narration and forget all about setting a scene. But honestly, where else would they be? It's been established that the kitchen TV is on the fritz.

"Maybe it won't matter," Francis says, "you scrubbed that thing clean, didn't you?"

"Yes."

"Then, so what if they know what killed him? Long as they can't trace it back to me. And why would they?"

Cassandra crosses her arms and pats her foot on the floor, noticing he's dressed for going out. "Where are you off to now?"

Francis shoots her a look. "I dunno. It's a beautiful morning, thought I might kill some more neighbors to pass the time. You don't like Mrs. Gardner much, do you?"

Cassandra feels something sink in her stomach, but she tries to shrug it off. "Very funny. Just, for the love of God, keep a low profile. You're lucky nobody was around to hear you declaring jihad on all our appliances."

Yes, that's the best thing about a girl holding another girl hostage in the local playground – the joneses are too tied up to hear your domestic shootout.

Francis agrees to behave, and Cassandra enters the kitchen, seduced by the aroma of French toast, where she first notices Henry's blackened face.

"What the hell happened to you?"

Henry doesn't look at her. Taking one's eyes off a frying pan is about as bad an idea as, well, letting a seven-year-old use a frying pan.

"I did what you asked," he says, "I burned everything Thomas had on Grandpa."

Cassandra sticks out her lower lip and nods. "Nice. Check you out. Doesn't answer my question though."

Henry turns off the stove. "Thomas wasn't happy about it."

"Ah." Cassandra opens the fridge and takes out a carton of milk. "Well, make sure to stay in the house, then. Don't want anyone thinking your dad beats you. Or worse, me."

"You do beat me."

"Well, yeah, but we don't have to advertise it." She takes a sip from the carton.

"What about Rocky? When can I get him back?"

Cassandra wipes her lips. "Right, him. Hm, wonder if he's still alive. I haven't checked once, if I'm honest, hope someone remembered to feed him."

Henry could probably use a pill to reduce his stress levels right now. "You promised!"

"I said *maybe*. Maybe? I don't know what I said anymore. Anyway, the deal was, you get the dog back when your cousins stop their investigating. Have they stopped?"

"Yes! I-I think so. Fred's gone, David stopped because of Rocky, and I don't know where Thomas is."

"What else did they have on Albert?"

"Uh, I think just a key?"

Cassandra's interest is piqued. "A key?"

"They thought it would open Grandpa's treasure chest."

It sounds so adventurous, doesn't it? 'Treasure chest.' So much better than 'drug money.' Francis sure feels the enthusiasm since he turns on his heels to eavesdrop by the kitchen door.

"Where is this chest?" Cassandra asks.

"I don't know!" Henry tells her, "I swear, I don't think anyone knows."

"Alright." Cassandra puts the empty carton back in the fridge. "Let's wait a couple more days then, see how this plays out. If things cool down, I'll think about bringing Rocky back."

Henry starts tearing up. Have we had a single episode in which he didn't cry? "Please! Tell me where he is, I won't get him out, I just wanna know he's eating and that he's safe!"

Cassandra smiles. "Henry, if I trusted you to do what you say, I wouldn't have had the dog taken in the first place."

Henry sits down, the redness of his cheeks showing through the blackened skin.

"Now," Cassandra reaches for a slice of toast, "get these over to Nana, she needs help with everything now. Oh, and remember to change her diaper every six hours. I never changed any of my own kids, I'll be damned if I start with an old woman."

She steals a bit of toast, bites into it and walks away. When she does, Francis is no longer in sight.

On her way out of the house, however, Cassandra finds Charlie, sat on the wall of her flowerbed, smoking a cigarette.

"Did you see what my son looks like?" he asks.

"Yeah. Poor thing, just when you thought he couldn't get uglier."

Wow. Charlie has to laugh because what else can he do? "You're unbelievable."

"Me? Last time I checked, *you* took his damn mutt."

Charlie gets up so quick it makes my head spin. "Because you told me to!"

"Yeah, well, if I don't take some initiative, I can't get anyone in this family to do anything. And we all know everything I do is for you kids *and* your own kids. But you're as much in it as I am, so don't come at me with a sermon, 'cause hypocrisy annoys me."

Charlie throws down his cigarette and steps on it. "Well then, give me what you promised."

Cassandra sneers. "Of course. So much for that high ground, huh? You are father of the year, right up to the moment booze is involved."

"I won't give you a sermon," he says, reaching out his hand, "but I won't take one from you either."

Cassandra sustains a sigh. Then, she opens her purse and takes out a keychain. "Here. Big one opens the door to Nate's restaurant; small one opens his warehouse. The beers are in the freezer."

Charlie snatches the keys and pockets them.

"See?" Cassandra says, with a smirk, "What won't I do for you kids?"

*

"Sources say the weapon used to kill Mr. Turner was unearthed next to the soccer field in Monastery. The person who found it was –"

You'd think Nicole would be more captivated by the recent developments in the latest unsolved murder in

Monastery, but her mind is elsewhere. Boy, that was a long-winded sentence. And no, her mind's not in her recent breakup with Fred, or David, or the shocking details of how that all happened. Her mind is on the pancakes; it *has* to be on the pancakes. They're the only thing keeping her from jumping over a cliff.

"What's that smell?" Celeste asks as she comes down the stairs, tying the robe around her. "Did you make breakfast?"

"I wanted to do something nice for you," Nicole says.

Celeste steps into the kitchen. "Honey, that's so sweet of you."

"You might change your tune once you try the pancakes. They keep sticking to the pan and burning."

Celeste smiles and takes the handle from her. "The trick is in the flick of the wrist. You just – *ow!*"

"Aunt Cel?"

For a moment there, Celeste forgot her wrist should not be flicked anytime soon. "I'm such an airhead," she says, wrapping her other hand around her throbbing bruise, "I forgot I hurt myself."

Nicole moves her aunt's hand and takes a look at her wrist. It's purple all around. "How'd you do this exactly?"

"I-I got my hand stuck the other day. Silly me, lost my balance reaching for a spoon and fell against the drawer."

"Did you put ice on it?"

"I did, and I'll do it again. Now, sit, sit, let's eat! These look positively yummy." They take their seats at the table and Celeste reaches for the chocolate spread. "Now, what spurred this random act of kindness?"

Nicole tries to think of what to say. "I guess I just wanna feel like I'm not a horrible person. Which I'm sure is a selfish reason for doing nice things, but here we are."

"Does this have to do with that Torrance girl?" Celeste asks.

"In part."

"I don't understand. She tied you down and threatened to hurt you, why would you be the horrible person in that scenario? By the way, did you ever call the police on her?"

Nicole cuts into her pancake. "And tell them what? 'Help, someone tried to maim me with plastic toys and tutti-frutti juice?'"

Celeste concedes. "Really though, why did she do that?"

Nicole breathes in before she lets out, "I cheated on Fred. With David. Which means David cheated on Erica. Kinda."

"I see." Celeste drinks some of her milk, trying to look inconspicuous.

Nicole honestly expected more of a reaction. A telling-off, perhaps? "So, yeah. That's why I need to do all I can to keep from feeling like the worst person in the world."

Celeste puts her glass down and holds her niece's hand. "You feel like a horrible person?"

Nicole nods. "I really do."

Celeste smiles. "Then that's a start, isn't it? Horrible people don't think they're horrible."

She resumes eating. As does Nicole, who mulls over what she's just head. There's some sense to the logic employed, that is certain.

Deep down, both women know the truth – that this is just what they must tell themselves to get through the day.

But, so long as it works, right?

*

"It appears the detective headlining the investigation into Mr. Turner's murder has yet to make an appearance on the site of the –"

You know when you dislike someone so much that everything they say annoys the hell out of you? That would be one of the reasons Walt's morning isn't off to a good start. But it's not just that Cora's disparaging him on local television – no, she could be talking about pruning flowers and it would still have him frothing out the mouth. It's also what he's dealing with at home.

"No, Rob, I know, I'm sorry," he says to the phone locked between his ear and shoulder, to Cora's husband, no less, "look, I've just got a lot on my plate at home, I'll be there when I can." He cuts into a piece of ham toast. "For God's sake, Rob, just hold the fort for a while! You always wanted to lead a case, so step up!"

He nearly slams the phone on the counter, then walks down the hall with the toast on a tray, next to a glass of OJ.

"I'm coming in with your breakfast," Walt announces, "so, no funny business."

With some difficulty, he unlocks the door to his sons' bedroom and pushes it forward. Thomas is sat on the lower bunk bed, his face rid of expression.

"I made your favorite," Walt says, "ham-and-cheese toast, no cheese."

He smiles as he says this. It's a running gag with the Fords, ever since Thomas was little and asked for such a thing.

"That never gets old," my grandson says.

Walt puts the tray down on the desk by the window. "Did you sleep well?"

Thomas looks at the door, which is now wide open. Walt's back is turned to him, but he's sat still in bed. The slightest movement would alert his police-trained father. Also, even if he managed to escape him, Monastery is fifteen miles away.

"Thomas?"

"Yeah, sure, I slept like a captive baby."

"I'm sorry I had to do this," Walt tells him. "It was a bit extreme, I know. I'm just trying to protect you."

"Why do I have to be confined to my room, though? Why not just keep me at home, free to move around?"

"Because if I did that, the moment I went to the bathroom, *you* would lock me in there to get out, or contact your cousins."

"Some trust you have in me."

"I know what I've raised." He starts walking out.

"Do you know what happened to my grandfather, though?"

The question acts as a barrier to Walt, keeping him in place.

"I take it that's a yes," Thomas says. "And you're an officer of the law. Someone who has the authority to arrest Grandpa's killer, yet you have done no such thing. Which leads me to believe whatever happened wasn't anyone's fault. That our family is not in any real danger. If that is the case, then – why can't I know?"

Walt looks at him. "You're just too young."

Thomas stands up. "Since *when*? My entire life, everyone has gone out of their way to say I am wise beyond my years, none louder or more proudly than you! Why is this the one thing I am too young for?"

"Because *I* am too young for it!" Walt shouts.

Thomas sits back down in confusion.

"Because I could never be old enough, wise enough, *anything* enough to handle this, Thomas! You want to know the truth so bad, and you don't know what it implicates!" He pauses. "It's a *disease*. It infests you, it takes over every part of you, it affects everything you do from here on out."

Thomas is stripped of arguments. What do you say to something like that?

"I'm glad your mother finally had the courage to tell me," Walt says. "I can't imagine what it was like for her, keeping it secret all these years. If you knew the things I look back on, all these weird reactions, little behaviors of hers that I could never understand and now make perfect sense to me. But dear God, Thomas, I wish I'd never known. And if you did find out, you'd wish the same."

Thomas looks up at him. "I *will* find out."

Walt slowly shakes his head. "Not if I can help it. Because long before you got be wise beyond your years, I swore I'd protect you with the rest of mine."

Walt breathes in and walks out, again.

"Even if I end up hating you?" Thomas says.

Walt puts his hand on the frame of the door and doesn't look back. The tear in his eye doesn't need exposing.

"I love you enough to let you hate me."

He leaves at last.

Making sure to lock up behind him.

*

I'm taking you from morning straight into the evening time, dear reader, simply because nothing else of note happened during the day.

The sky is dark and ominous as always. The men have ambled back home from the bars; the women have taken their roasts out of the oven; the children have glued their faces to phones, laptops, and other gadgets of the like. But over at the Childs place, there's no activity whatsoever. Since they've moved back to the country, rare is the day when David's family all sit down to break bread. When your mother runs the most successful restaurant in the tri-county area, it leaves her little time to cook for just her kin.

Or, to tend to her beloved son. The one sitting alone in the dark living room. The light of the bathroom is on, for whatever reason, and passes through the semi-open doors, but the TV turned off by itself minutes ago, even if the warning message counted down the seconds right before David's eyes.

It's nine p.m. Usually, around this time, David would fire up VH1. Tonight, they're doing a Michael Jackson retrospective. He should be up dancing, singing, making Madam Witch plug up her ears next door. But David's living in a 'Thriller' of his own, which makes him feel so 'Bad' he can't even recognize the 'Man in the Mirror' anymore.

Yes, those were terrible. Am I sorry? Never.

Things have taken an unexpected turn for David. A couple days ago, he dreaded going to sleep, knowing his Rocky-led nightmares would haunt him. Now, thanks to Henry's necklace, he's sleeping like an angel. So, the nightmare doesn't begin until his eyes blast open.

There's a faint tapping at the door, which soon becomes a scratching. David's head turns slightly to the right, but the sound barely courses through his numbness. When it does, he jumps up from the couch, his heart restlessly hopeful.

"Rocky!" he says, opening the door.

Not Rocky. Just his friend.

"Oliver." David gives the black Labrador a bittersweet smile as he bends down to rub his face. "How are you, buddy?"

Oliver – Rocky's friend from episode 3, if you need reminding – whines softly, his snout pointed down. Rocky hasn't come out to play in the longest time, so he's starting to worry.

"Aw, I miss him too," David says, scratching behind the dog's ears, "have you been looking for him?"

Oliver wags his tail as if to reply. I can confirm he has; sadly, though, Oliver has never ventured past the school, and the arena is a ways out from that.

"We'll find him, buddy, soon. I – I need to get out there too. Stop moping around, actually do something."

David looks up and sighs. Then his eyes both widen and sadden at the night sky. "No."

His heart fills with despair, yet again. Coupled with overbearing fear.

It's a full moon tonight.

*

For many a millennium now, full moons have been associated with bizarre or insane behavior. Monastery is no different. Every generation there grew up on the same tall tales, of witches' rituals, gruesome murders, and yes, animalistic transformations, all influenced by the moon. Of course, based on everything you've seen so far in this story, you could easily assume a full moon always hangs above town. That, or something in the water's making everyone a little gaga.

But I commend my youngest grandson for maintaining his sanity in these trying times. Rocky wasn't given so much as a toy to play with. Day in and day out, all he's got to look at are the rundown white walls of the pen, the rusty metal door, the hung weight that operates it, plus the food and water bowls. On any given night, he'd be tucked in with David on his couch, sharing a bowl of popcorn, watching *Desperate Housewives* reruns. David's a Susan, Rocky is obviously Gabrielle.

It's these little moments you look back on when your life is turned upside down, isn't it? Rocky would actually give his ear for one more leisurely night like that.

The moon looks bigger and shinier than ever before. Rocky looks up at it and tries to part his jaws, hoping to break off the muzzle, but all he does is hurt his snout. Oh, to howl at the moon again, in that beautiful soprano of his!

He closes his eyes and imagines it. He's out there in the world, running amok, greeting his neighbors with a polite bark. Stopping just short of a precipice, looking up at the moon and –

Owoooooooooooooooo!!!

Um. Yes, exactly. Except Rocky didn't do that – he couldn't have.

It sounded so distant and so close, all at once. What is it they say about the werewolf? If you hear it next to you, that means it's far away; if you hear it in the distance, then it's right behind you. That myth isn't much help in this moment.

But the thumping sound of a large foot hitting the sand, now that was nearby. A little *too* nearby. Rocky backs into the corner of the pen; he squeals a little at first, then keeps it in, but his shivering increases by the second, as the footsteps draw closer and closer. Remnants of dust and sand creep below the door, followed by a foul stench, the likes of which his pink little nose had never detected.

Owoooooooooooooooo!!!

This one sounded so distant. Like it came from the next town over.

That can't be good.

The door is pounded on. Every knock, if you can call it that, is accompanied by a puff that heats up an already scorching night. Rocky buries his tiny head in his paws and prepares to accept his fate. From pet to prey.

The door is brought up a few millimeters. The hot air slides through, nauseating, disorienting. Like rotten flesh lodged between unwashed teeth.

Can you call it an analogy if that's literally what it is?

A large, hairy brown paw peeks below the door. Rocky uncovers one eye as the massive limb slides the metal upwards like a receding guillotine.

What he sees next nearly makes his heart stop.

The legends don't do the Monastery Werewolf justice. Each generation adds something new to the description, but no one's come close to accurately portraying the beast. Its eyes are an undocumented shade of yellow, the irises circled by bloodshot lines. Its teeth grow in size and sharpness from the corners of its mouth towards the center, culminating in five-inch fangs which are covered in a gooey, brown substance. Its tail could storm up hurricanes if wagged, and its paws could fill up the trenches in the Old Farm, each toe as a big as a toddler's head. In fact, it appears the soil lowers beneath the creature's paws every time it steps forward.

Rocky cries tears of terror when faced with a beast that could swallow him whole in a fraction of a second. His eyes peer into the thing's own, and linger in them for a while, evoking mercy.

Until they don't. Wait a minute…

Oh. Hello there.

The monster's eyes soften, and it soon lies on its stomach, raising up another cloud of dust.

Rocky shakes his tail and barks happily. Honestly, what was the need for that mighty scare? Quite rude, if you asked him. Could have just said who it was.

The werewolf curls up at the opposite corner of the pen and Rocky moves to join it, snuggling up against its fur. The two fall fast asleep, finding comfort in their reunion.

So nice to be with family again.

***

Act 2

A new day has come, and not in the harmonious Céline Dion way, since David has done the unthinkable this morning – he got up before seven a.m. Earlier than his parents, even! He had his usual chocolate flakes, brushed his teeth, put on his red shirt, red shorts and red flip-flops (don't worry, they all get washed regularly), picked up the 'missing dog' posters, and headed for the door. But his mother stopped him just as his hand grabbed the knob.

"Honey?"

"Oi."

Maggie rubs her eyes as she comes out of her room in a summer robe. "What're you doing up so early?"

"Gonna go look for Rocky. Bye." He opens the door.

"David, wait."

"What?"

She grabs him by the shoulders and quickly runs her mind for excuses to keep him home. The only thing she thinks to say is, 'Rocky's fine, he's in the arena, he's getting looked after, I'll bring him home soon.' Then she thinks of all the follow-up questions he would ask, and how she would absolutely have no answers for them.

"Mom?"

Maggie snaps out of it. She's been staring blankly at him all the while.

"Good luck," she says, before kissing him on the forehead.

Off he goes.

Mr. Arnold, who's been known as 'Uncle Scrooge' for many a decade now, finally splurged on air-conditioning this summer, and quickly reaped the benefits of said investment. All the locals from both Hovel Street and the new housing complex by the church like to spend their afternoons at Arnold's, wetting their lips with a cold brewski. But David doesn't drink, so that's not what he's after.

He places a flyer on the counter soon as he comes in. "Mr. Arnold?"

"David!" the old man greets as he puts away dirty coffee cups. "Rocket popsicle?"

"No, Mr. Arnold, I was wondering if I could leave this here, Rocky's gone missing. Also, yes, a rocket popsicle."

Mr. Arnold dries his hands on a rag and takes the poster. "Oh, I heard about this. Your mom, she made it public knowledge at your uncle's the other day. How long's it been since he went missing?"

"Going on a week now."

Mr. Arnold breathes through his teeth as he reaches in the freezer for a popsicle. "Oh, so long. Son, I don't mean to tell you to give up hope, but the longer it takes, the less likely it is him turning up. Maybe he's been taken in by a nice family?"

"No, he's being held hostage as a bargaining chip."

"Ah. Um, I-I'll put up the flyer."

David takes the popsicle from him. "Thank you, Mr. Arnold. Oh, my cousin Fred is also M.I.A., if you happen to see him —"

Mr. Arnold points behind David. "Isn't that him there?"

David turns around to see Fred poking his head through the ribbon curtain at the door.

"Fred? Fred!"

Upon seeing his cousin, Fred immediately darts off.

"Fred!" David rushes after him, popsicle at hand.

"David!" Mr. Arnold calls, "You need to pay for that!"

Fred sprints down Hovel Street like he's off to save someone from getting hung, and David chases right after, calling his name.

"Fred! Wait, slow down! I don't have a lot of stamina!"

No such luck, Fred even quickens his step. The top portion of the popsicle comes off the stick and hits David in the face.

"Fred, please! Stop in the name of love!"

Fred's nearly reached the playground when his foot lands funny. "Argh!"

He sits down in the middle of the road and takes off his sneaker, allowing David to catch up with him. By the time he does, his t-shirt is stained with all colors of the rocket.

"Jesus," David says between pants, "I got donkey pains."

That's what we in town call those sharp abdominal pains you get after a quick jog. We have a fun vocabulary, don't we?

Fred rubs his sprained ankle. "What do you want?"

"Where have you been? We haven't heard from you in days, where are you staying?"

"What do you care?"

"Fred, please! I know you hate me right now; you have every right to, but everyone's worried sick."

"Like who?" he spits. "Grandma kicked me out! My mom won't answer my calls, my dad opened my texts and didn't reply! My girlfriend cheated on me, and then there's *you*!"

David nearly backs away, out of instinct.

Fred brings his hands to his face. "God. How could you, David? You were my best friend."

"I was?"

Oh, David.

He said it instinctively, no harm meant. But it felt like another knife through Fred's heart.

"I-I mean," David tries, "I'm so sorry, I –"

"Save it." Fred puts his shoe back on and tries to get up.

David moves towards him again. "Fred, I'm sorry. I know saying that doesn't change anything, I can't even imagine how you feel right now, but I meant it when I said I would make it up to you, so let me! Come back home, you, you can even take my bed, I'll sleep on the couch!"

"I can fend for myself."

"You don't have to."

"No?" Fred looks away to give the tears a chance to retreat. "You wanna know how I feel right now? *Alone*, David. And that's how I wanna be."

"Fred."

"Leave me. Alone."

David backs off, defeated. Watching his cousin as he walks away with a limp.

Then he realizes he may as well throw the popsicle away.

*

No popsicles for Rick today, which might be a good thing, considering what happened the last time he got one. But all he's got to eat this morning is enough cereal to fill up just one third of a bowl. His father forgot to hit the store, again. Oh, wait, he didn't – there's four new packs of beer bottles in the fridge. Maybe Rick should have himself a liquid breakfast?

Mutt waddles in, his lips around one said bottle. Yes, because he doesn't get his beer in cans, as we've plainly seen – he thinks the metal gives it a weird taste. In my day, drunks weren't so picky; booze could have come out of a goat's rear end and we would line up behind it.

"I got nothing to eat," Rick says.

"What's that got to do with me? You're fat enough as it is."

Fat? If Rick turns sideways you can't see him anymore.

"Ya forgot to get me my cereal," he says, banging the box on the table, "not that it matters 'cause we got no milk, couldn't eat it with yer damn beer, now could I?"

I've tried that once, on a dare. Do not recommend it.

Mutt puts down his empty bottle and brings his face closer to his son's. Then lets out an almighty burp that burns Rick's nose hairs, as well as mine – they weren't kidding when they said heat rises. He backs away, laughing hysterically as he opens the fridge to fetch another beer.

Before he can even realize what he's doing, Rick's tossed the empty bottle at his father, hitting him square in the forehead. Mutt goes down like a rock, probably because his balance wasn't that sturdy to begin with.

He winds up in the corner between the wall and the washer. He then runs his hand on his forehead and sees the blood on his fingertips. "Son of a —"

Rick can hardly believe he just did that, but there's no time to think about it. The lines on his father's face quickly denounce the change in his mood, from playful to pissed. Rick jumps over Mutt and out of the kitchen, headed for the door. Mutt – I kid you not – actually roars, getting back up with a jump and dashing after his son. Rick runs out but quickly turns back around, stopping in the plaza and facing the house. His father emerges at the door like a lion ready to pounce, but the presence of his neighbors gives him literal pause.

"You wanna smack me around, huh, big man?" Rick shouts. "Do it out here!! Come on, I dare ya, I double dare ya, take yer belt off, *Dad*!!"

In the patio of Starla's café, Horace and Della Towers look up from their cups of espresso. Perry Lawson stops bouncing his basketball below the schoolyard, and Janice Penshaw puts her phone call on hold, mere meters from the father and son.

"Come on! Show everyone you's a tough guy!"

Mutt rests his hands over his waist, defeated. His lips pursed, his gaze lethal. The nerve on that little twat.

Rick spreads his arms as if saying, 'Well?' The neighbors, meanwhile, admire the spectacle. I'd like to say that's concern in their eyes, but for the most part it's excitement.

Mutt stares at his son through detesting eyes, almost salivating. He's not a lion anymore, just a rabid dog looking at a cat that's gone up a tree. He turns around and heads back inside, slamming the door behind him.

Rick pants, then looks around at all the passers-by. "Show's over, folks."

*

David comes home after a while. All the posters have been handed out, which feels like futile effort upon reflection. Not only does everyone in town know exactly who Rocky is and what he looks like, but he's certainly not being kept where he can be found.

He did it, though. He took the initiative to do something other than sit on his bummed-out butt. Though that is of little comfort.

He takes out his wallet and phone, placing them on the black picnic table, and the Beatles' 'Help' starts ringing out. Francis calling.

Has Francis ever called him?

"Hello?"

"David! My favorite nephew!"

Weirder and weirder. "What's up?"

On the other side of the call, Francis bears the creepiest grin, as is his wont. "Look, I know you've been a bit down lately, since Rocky went missing, but I got good news for you."

David's eyes become full-on circles. "You found Rocky?!"

"You could say that. But here, let him tell you."

David awaits with bated breath to hear his buddy again. But when Rocky's screeches come through the phone and escalate into loud squawks, David's breath is sucked out of him. It's like his chest has taken a pounding.

Back in the arena, Francis removes his foot from Rocky's tail, leaving his boot print on it.

"There. Don't you feel better?" he says to the phone.

The rage in David's eyes pushes his tears out. "You monster! You took him!"

"Again, you could say that, but it's never quite as simple, is it? But it can be, from now on. I have something you want – you have something I need."

David tries to calm down, even if his cheeks already hurt from all the sudden crying. "What?"

"Little bird told me you kids found a key. I think we all know what it would have been used on."

"So, it's true. You've been looking for Grandpa's money."

"Hey, I'm an heir after all. Slosh had the nerve to die and leave us nothing, I'm entitled to whatever's in that chest."

What about my five other kids then? They're left to suck on their thumbs?

"So, be a good boy, bring the key to Unkie Francis, will you?"

"I, I don't have it, Thomas does!"

"I know," Francis says, "and here's the thing, I could have called Thomas, almost did, but then I thought – would he have given me the key for Rocky?"

David feels another pounding on his chest.

"You and I know the answer to that, don't we?" Francis says. "Feeling pretty grateful I called you now, aren't you?"

David doesn't know what to say anymore.

"So. Get the key. Call me when you do, and I'll let you know where we can make the exchange. Deal?"

Below him, Rocky balls up into a corner of the pen, keeping his sobs to a minimum.

Meanwhile, a tiny puddle of David's tears has formed on the living room floor. "Deal," he says.

"See, David? This is why you're my favorite."

Francis hangs up.

David sits down on the couch. His insides are numb; his outside is sore from the crying.

My grandson's mind starts racing like usual, but he can't let it do that. Focus, David. All you need to do is get the key. How hard can it be?

All you must do is steal it from Thomas. Never let him know.

But – where is Thomas?

*

Thomas' palm is red all over from the incessant banging on his door, and Walt's headache increases with every thud, but neither one is letting up in this ordeal. The older Ford stays at home still, foregoing work and all other responsibilities; the younger one rebels still, determined to make his captor's life as unbearable as his own.

Until the final straw breaks the detective's back.

"KNOCK IT OFF!"

The punch that accompanies the bellowed command is so violent that Thomas is nearly pushed on his back.

"You're not getting out of there till you give up this crap about your grandfather," Walt shouts through the door. "So you better stop what you're doing, Thomas, or I swear to God your next meal will be laced with enough sedatives to put down an army!"

Thomas puffs, not yet beat. "Where's Mom in all this? Did she give you the okay to keep your child locked up?"

"She's at work."

"She *works*?!"

I'm surprised as well.

"And yeah," Walt resumes, "she's fine with this." He guffaws. "You know, I didn't understand why she was so gung-ho about bringing you back a few weeks ago. Now I do."

"You sure catch on slow for a detective," Thomas says, "I mean, you were married to Mom how long? Yet you never suspected a thing."

Yikes. Talk about pushing it.

"I wonder what your cop friends would say if they knew," he's not done yet? "Better yet, what would they think of you keeping me here?"

"Have fun trying to tell them." Walt pats the door twice.

Thomas kneels against the door. "I also wonder what Mom would say if she knew Mrs. Leeds made a pass at you the other day."

Walt freezes. Not just his body, his brain – it loses all ability to think.

But Thomas isn't done. "Another testament to your capacities as a detective. I was hiding behind the bushes just five feet from the both of you, yet you were none the wiser. Imagine my surprise when she started fondling your chest."

Walt's headache slides down his throat and blocks it.

"The things she was saying – do the two of you have history? Is Mom aware?"

Walt finally speaks, so lowly it barely makes it through the door. "There's no history. She came on to me, I rejected her. Simple."

That devilish grin of my grandson's rears its head again. I did not miss it. "Yes, well, I'm a child, as you so often like to remind me. My memory is unreliable. You better hope I remember that detail when I tell Mom that Cora Leeds had her hands all over you by the stream."

This time, Thomas is literally pushed over when the door opens and hits him. Walt comes in like a raging bull and grabs his son by the collar, so quickly he doesn't have time to scream.

"Memorize this, you little prick! You can screw up my marriage, you can tell my friends whatever you want, you can stab me in the gut and twist the knife and I would bleed out here *loving you with all that I am!*"

He drops his son on the bed and Thomas lowers his head into his shoulders, like a turtle recoiling to its shell.

Walt moves closer to his face. "But until you do any of that, I will do everything in my power to make a *decent man* out of you. Something I have clearly failed at so far."

He walks out again, slamming the door behind him. I think he fears what might happen if he sticks around.

Thomas falls to his knees by the bedside and buries his sniveling face in the sheet. His sobbing goes on for a while, as it dawns on him that the consequences for his actions are getting graver by the minute.

You'd think this would be enough to stop him. Get him to take a step back, do some critical introspection, and realize his determination to solve my death has made his life a torment.

But in this moment, his determination morphs into desperation. And you know what they say about desperate times.

Thomas joins his hands over the mattress and closes his eyes, about to do something he never thought he would.

"I-I know I have had my doubts about you. I know I have been skeptical, derisive. I have shown reluctance to, to believe what you are capable of, even when presented with evidence. I am sorry. I am so sorry for all of that, I hope you can forgive me. And if you are there, if you can hear me, please, *please* help me, Madam Witch!"

Fifteen miles away, Madam Witch puts down her utensils and sits back in her chair, away from her stew.

"Ah... They always call during dinner."

*

The moon is no longer full tonight. A quick Google search tells me this is the waning gibbous phase, whatever that means, but the point is we can look forward to a peaceful night, thankfully.

Fred sets up camp by sprawling down two sheets on the grass, one on top of the other. He's spent the last couple nights at the bust stop on Cutthroat Cross, till the cops made him move. So tonight, he's sleeping under the stars. That's alright, he's always wanted to camp out. Not long ago, he and Henry had joked about sleeping out on the front yard when it got too hot in their room. But there's no Henry around. There's nobody whatsoever.

So he thinks.

He uses the bags with his belongings as pillows, having sold most of his stuff already. Then he takes out a Snickers bar he managed to get at Starla's, after his failed attempt at buying crisps at Mr. Arnold's. Stupid David.

The phone rings. Mom! Mom's calling, finally! He slides the little green button up, brings the phone to his ear, and of course the battery dies at that very moment. I don't know what you expected - unless you skipped the credits, you'd know Tara's not in this episode.

Fred puts the phone down on his lap. This would be one of those moments where you just have to laugh. He doesn't though.

Well, then. Early bedtime it is. He'll figure out how to charge his phone tomorrow.

Fred lies on his side, his hands under his face to keep the stuff in the bags from hurting him as he sleeps. He hits his head on the wall of the arena as he adjusts himself, but he pays it no mind – just a bump.

On the other side of the wall, Rocky thinks he's heard something. He stands in wait of a follow-up noise, but nothing comes, so he lets his guard down.

And so, with a beautiful, starry night above them and a thick, white wall between them, my two grandsons go to sleep.

***

Act 3

Today is an important day.

Alfie doesn't know it yet, so he goes about it like any other. First a shower, then getting dressed, and ultimately styling his hair the usual way, with the fringe drooping down the side, partially covering his left eye. Followed by the same bowl of oatmeal for breakfast, by himself once more – dad's off investigating a murder, mom's off reporting on it. Even the episode of his favorite cartoon (the one he doesn't let his friends know he still watches) is a repeat. Everything about this day seems ordinary. Until –

Knock! Knock!

Probably Caesar, asking if they're going to the pool or not. Alfie opens the door, and his nonchalance quickly turns to surprise.

"Madam Witch?"

She's smiling. She doesn't often smile, does she?

"Morning."

"Uh, can I help you?"

Her hands remain behind her back. "It's come to my attention that your friend is in trouble. Thomas, I mean. He's being held captive in his own home, back in the city. I figured you should know."

Alfie crosses his arms. "Why?"

"Well, I'm a busy woman, I can't help him. Someone should, though."

Alfie bites his underlip. "I don't care about Thomas."

Madam Witch's smile becomes a scornful smirk. "Oh. My mistake, then."

With no vestige of farewell, she turns around and walks on. Alfie furrows his brows in puzzlement before closing the door.

Back to the oatmeal then, and Cuddly Wuddly Bear on TV. The pool is a good idea, sure, he'll text Caesar back to say they can go. He should take the orange trunks this time; the white ones always get grass stains which –

Damn it.

He drops his spoon in the bowl and runs out of the house.

Stupid Thomas.

Knock! Knock!

Alfie shakes his head as he waits for the door to open, as if scolding himself for putting in the effort. As if Thomas deserves it after shutting him off all summer long, coming to him only when he needed something. But Alfie's better than that, highway all the way.

The door opens, and Alfie looks down. "Hey. So, um, I think Thomas is in trouble. We should probably do something to help."

Below him, Martin puts his hands on his hips and grins.

"You came to the wight pewson."

*

Joanna Spyder, now in her early sixties, used to run a café in Monastery, in the place that is now a mechanic's office. When she gave up her business, she started a cab service; she figured the local elders could use a way of getting from point A to point B, be that to get their groceries, their prescriptions, or to visit their loved ones. Imagine her surprise when her first customers of the day turn out to be a pair of young boys, and point B turns out to be the city.

"Just keep the meter running, Mrs. Spyder," Alfie says, as he and Martin get out of the green Opel that she put a cab light over.

The Fords live in a condo in the suburbs of the city, Portalegrum. Needless to say, Martin doesn't have his own key, so they must stand in wait outside the building until an unsuspecting neighbor comes by.

"Pwease help," Martin tells the lady. "We got locked out."

"Aw, you poor thing," the woman says, as she fumbles for her keys while juggling two grocery bags.

"Let me get those," Alfie says.

Before long, both kids are inside. "Ready?" Alfie asks, handing Martin his cell phone.

"Bitch, pwease."

Walt enters his son's room with a sheet of paper in his hands. "I printed out your, um, your grandfather's letter."

"Did you now?" Thomas says, stoically. He's sat on the bed with his hands between his knees, avoiding eye contact.

Walt leans against the desk. "So, first things first, who was he writing to?"

Thomas shrugs his shoulders. "I would not know. I presumed it was a mistress."

"Alright. What's this money he's talking about?"

"Grandpa was involved in some wrongdoings during his smuggling days. Surely, you have heard of that."

Walt nods. "I have. So, you think that's related? To his death?"

Another shrug. "He certainly thought it would be."

Walt almost sighs with relief. It's better if his son also thinks that.

"The woman who told him he would die, who is –?"

A ringtone rings out from his pocket. A ringtone rings out – what a dumb thing to say. Walt takes out his cell. "It's your brother."

"Yay."

Walt leaves the room, his printout staying behind. "Hey, champ, what's going on?" He remembers to lock up, though.

"Daddy! I need my bike, can you pwease bwing it over?"

Great, just what he needed. "Now's not a good time, Martin."

Martin stomps his foot on the hallway of the building, which unnerves Alfie – what if Walt can hear them?

"Pwease! All the kids are doing a bike wace today and I can't join!"

Walt really wishes he'd gotten a vasectomy now. "Fine. I'll see what I can do."

"Can you check to see if the bwakes awe fine?"

"Martin, I did that last month."

"Daddy!"

Walt slaps his forehead. "God, alright! I'll do it now."

He walks out of his apartment, this time not bothering to lock the front door, and heads towards the garage of the building. Alfie and Martin peek from around the elevator and make their move, walking on tiptoes.

"Thank you," Martin says, "you're the best daddy ever."

"Yeah, yeah."

Inside the apartment, Martin realizes how little he's missed being home, while Alfie calls for Thomas, in as low an invocation as he can muster.

"Alfie?!"

Thomas can hardly believe his hears, which he's got pressed to the door. Alfie unlocks it and Thomas lunges himself at him. The printout of my letter is now in his hand.

"What are you doing here?!" Thomas asks.

"Madam Witch said you were in trouble."

Thomas raises his brows. "Wow. That truly was worth the shot."

"We have to go fast, your dad will be back soon."

Down the hall, Thomas sees his little brother on the phone, and can't help but feel a teeny bit proud.

"Daddy, are you sure it's wo'king? Twy it again."

"Martin, I can't very well sit on a training bike and ride it!"

"If you loved me, you would!"

In the garage, Walt has reached his limit. "Son, you know what, if you're so worried about getting in an accident, then you should just not go on that race. Since when do three-year-olds do bike races anyway?"

"But —"

"Goodbye, champ." He hangs up.

Back at the apartment, all Martin can say is, "Uh-oh."

"We have to get out, stat!" Alfie says.

"Wait! He's going to know I'm gone; he'll chase after us!"

"Just lock the door again!"

"I've been banging on that door nonstop for hours, if all of a sudden I stop, he will know something is amiss."

A conundrum indeed. How to solve this?

Both friends turn their heads to the little man down the hall. Martin lets out a dramatic sigh.

"What would you two bwains do without me?"

Thomas and Alfie rush out, missing Walt in the hall by a nail. They get inside the cab and tell Mrs. Spyder to hit he gas.

"I can't believe you came all this way," Thomas tells his friend, "I thought you hated me."

"Yeah, well, I spend most of my time hating you, then I hate myself for that, and it's just way too much hate, know what I mean?"

"I really don't but thank you."

"Also, I'm gonna waste my entire allowance on the cab fare, so you had better pay me back."

"Of course!"

"Another thing," Alfie reaches for a folder he'd left in the backseat, "I brought you something."

Thomas takes it from him. "What's this?"

"After you left my house the other day, I was bit by the curiosity bug, did my own research on Mom's laptop. To see what I could find on your grandfather."

"I thought I had covered everything," Thomas says, opening the file.

"You forgot to look up one name in her database."

"Which one?"

Alfie arches his brows. "Cassandra Keane."

A confused Thomas looks down at the sheet on his lap. Looks like a medical record from the Portalegrum hospital, an old one at that. No stamp anywhere.

"I don't know how much help this can be," Alfie says, "but, it seems your grandmother had an abortion in the early eighties. Back when they weren't exactly legal."

Thomas puffs out. Great.

Another piece of the puzzle that won't fit with all the others.

*

Home sweet home. Well, home away from home, I suppose. Either way, Thomas feels a great rush when his feet hit Monastery soil once more. They get off at the end of Hovel Street and Alfie pays Mrs. Spyder her due.

"Hey, look," Alfie says, "someone's moving in next to your grandparents."

"That's nice," Thomas says, brushing off the moving truck at the end of the street.

"Where are we going?" Alfie asks.

"I want to do something at my grandma's place that I will need your help with."

Up the street they go, until a familiar voice calls out. "Thomas?"

"Godpa?"

David looks at him with a mixture of confusion and relief. "Where have you been?"

"It is a rather long story, and I am a little pressed for time. We shall catch up later."

David feels a sting of bitterness at this, and so does Alfie – it's all too familiar for him. But David gets over it fast. "Wait!"

"What is it?"

He moves closer to his Godson. "I'm sorry. For taking this whole Rocky thing out on you."

Thomas is stumped. "No, um, I was out of line."

David moves in for a hug. Thomas doesn't really know how to react, but gives in. It feels oddly comforting.

When it's broken off, they part with a smile. Thomas and Alfie rush up the street; David watches them go.

When they're good and away, David opens his palm and looks at the key. The words 'Chubby Chester' glisten in the sunlight.

*

"Come on!"

"Urgh!"

"Use your back!"

It takes a considerable amount of effort, but Thomas and Alfie manage to move the fridge out of its place – Fred made it seem so easy. They leave the fridge where it now blocks the access to the pantry, but everyone in that house can do without their daily share of rat-bitten crackers.

There's a square on the floor where the fridge used to be, drawn in the blackest possible mold. A spiderweb was torn apart in the process, there's stains on the tile that can never be scrubbed off, but what Thomas came to find is right there, in the middle of a green potato fry and a dead cockroach: evidence.

He carefully picks up a shard from the body of a wine bottle, with the label still on. It's nearly colorless and the wordings have almost been erased, but Thomas can still make out what it once read: Montecito, batch of 1973.

A couple, smaller bits of the same bottle are on the floor. One has a faint tint of red on a corner.

My grandson grins almost too vainly. It's the most validating experience when he's right about a hunch, even if it means the tale of my death gets grimmer and grimmer.

"What's that?" Alfie asks.

Thomas holds up the piece of glass for him to see. "Not long ago, we had a family lunch. My dad was elated to open a bottle of this wine and Pop Dennis recounted how he had given my grandpa the same wine, for when my mom got married. My dad asked her what happened to it then, and she froze. I knew there and then the bottle had something to do with my grandpa's death."

Alfie takes the shard from him and inspects it. "So, you think –"

"This is the murder weapon. My grandpa was killed with a bottle of wine."

Finally. The reader's known that since episode 1.

Alfie hands him back the piece. "I marvel at your deduction skills."

Let's marvel at how no one's cleaned below that fridge in fourteen years. No wonder they get so many rats.

"My skills are not as sharp as they might seem," Thomas tells him. "We also found a bloodied toy car below this fridge, and I have not the slightest clue how that connects to everything else."

"Maybe your grandpa was killed by a kid. Francis? How old was he then?"

"I am not ruling that out," Thomas says.

"Who's there?"

Nana's croaky voice reaches the kitchen. All this fridge-moving commotion woke her from her nap.

Thomas walks to Henry's bedroom. "Nana?"

Her head's facing the door, just the way she likes. "Hi, dear. What time is it?"

Thomas quickly checks his wristwatch. "Um, eleven-fifteen. What are you doing here?"

"You haven't heard."

Thomas moves closer. "Heard what?"

What they do hear is the front door opening. Crap.

Nana sees the worry in her nephew's eyes and says, "The window."

She watches as Thomas and Alfie jump out said window and rush off. I guess the fridge is staying where they left it.

"You think she'll tell on us?" Alfie asks, when they're out on the street.

To which Thomas says, "I'm choosing to believe she will not."

They're not in the clear yet, though – is that Charlie driving up the road? Thomas pulls at Alfie's arm and drags him through the nearest open door: Mr. Arnold's bar.

"Hey!" "Hurry!"

Inside, my grandson breathes a sigh of relief. This is starting to look like one of those black-and-white, police-robber comedies with the chase sequences.

"Can I help you boys?" Mr. Arnold asks from behind the counter.

Alfie figures they might as well give the man some clientele and asks for a couple sodas.

"You don't have to do that," Thomas says.

"Just pay me back when you find the treasure, I guess. Along with the cab fare."

Thomas smiles. Then wonders to himself where I might have hidden the 'treasure' indeed. And why everything about me, both life and death, is a never-ending mystery.

You know when you think so much about something that it's like you start seeing it wherever you go? No, that's never happened to me either. But imagine Thomas' surprise when he looks ahead and sees my – ahem – 'handsome' face, mere inches from his own.

His hand reaches out to the same picture we've seen before, me and George Turner at the fishing competition, the one he won from beneath me. Thomas puts his index finger over my face, which I think he intended as a symbolic gesture of affection, but ended up covering my whole mug, like he's trying to phase me out. It does feel nice, though; for once, Thomas comes across something pertaining to me that he doesn't immediately scrutinize.

While Alfie pays for the sodas, Thomas follows the hung pictures on the walls. So much history of Monastery portrayed within those small, wooden frames. A lavish wedding at the old church, before it crumbled to the ground. A bullfight witnessed by hundreds of euphoric spectators. Even a high school poetry competition, its winner shown receiving a medal up on a stage.

A seventeen-year-old Celeste Colm.

A seventeen –

Poetry...

Celeste.

The picture blurs into nothingness faster than you can say, 'Eureka!' Thomas takes a step back and reaches for support, but there's nothing to hold on to.

The pieces of the puzzle join their hands. They form a circle and dance around his head, but they no longer mock him, not this time – they sing him praise.

"I know everything," he says to himself.

I want to give poor Alfie a hug when he turns around and Thomas is nowhere to be seen.

KNOCK! KNOCK!

The knocks quickly become pounds; the pounds become cannonballs. Thomas' anxiousness to get to the bottom of things nearly makes him blow Celeste's door away. When Nicole opens it, he almost falls on their hallway.

"Thomas, what the hell?"

"WHERE IS YOUR AUNT?!"

Nicole almost jumped from the scare, but he pushed her away before she got the chance to.

"Miss Colm?! Miss Colm!!"

Celeste steps out of the kitchen, mittens around her hands. "Thomas, what is happening?"

Nicole starts shutting the door. "You can't just barge in like –"

Her thought is interrupted by Alfie coming in with a pair of sodas. "Thomas! What are you doing?"

Oh, they're all about to discover. Thomas puffs out his chest, in anticipation.

"Miss Colm, I shall waste no time dancing around the subject. My cousins and I have spent the last few months trying to solve our grandfather's apparent murder, and all the while, someone has either tried to help us or throw us off track by way of sending us increasingly cryptic poems, all signed, 'Albert'."

He pauses, and I do believe he does so for dramatic effect.

"I have an educated hunch *you* are that someone."

Gasp!

Shock and awe!

Who – what – why?!

None of that from Celeste, though. You'd expect her eyes to widen at this accusation, her jaw to drop, her chest to heave. Nothing of the sort happens.

Nicole crosses her arms and scoffs. "What? Okay, this is getting out of hand, you're losing your damn –"

Celeste holds up her hand before her niece can finish.

When Nicole notices the guilty look on her face, she's almost numbed. "Aunt Cel?"

Celeste moves to her armchair, slowly, under Thomas' accusing eyes. She removes the mittens from her hands and places them on the armrest.

Nicole walks towards her. "Aunt Cel, is he – did you send those poems?"

Celeste closes her eyes, bites the inside of her lip, and nods her head. Before her, three children experience different levels of perplexity. Nicole can't understand how her aunt might be involved in the mystery. Thomas doesn't get what her intent was behind those notes. Alfie plain doesn't know what the f___ is going on.

Nicole sits next to her aunt and takes her hand, hoping to seem sympathetic, even if the bewilderment stuns her. "Aunt Cel, why? Why did you do that? How did you even know what we were doing?"

"Because she was Grandpa's mistress," Thomas says. "Were you not?"

Nicole's jaw descends just a little more. She doesn't yet know how low it can drop, but she'll find out soon enough.

Thomas takes out my letter – the new version – from his pocket. "In fact, I believe he wrote this to you. Shortly before he passed."

Celeste takes the printout from him.

"The quality is far from ideal; I fear Henry burned the original. But it is still legible."

That it is. My lover's eyes well up when she instantly recognizes my handwriting – plus the true and original signature.

Celeste wipes her nose. "I wish I knew what to say."

Thomas sits down on the armchair across from her. "May I suggest the truth, from the beginning? It would be such a welcome change."

The truth. Of course. Celeste feels a burgeoning lump in her throat. The truth is caught in it, yearning to break free.

Ready to make everything worse.

She sits back and looks directly at Thomas, who waits impatiently, legs crossed. Nicole puts her bare feet up on the couch, holding her knees, and Alfie sits on the armrest beside Thomas, the sodas getting warm in his hands. All three with curious heads, all three staring at the middle-aged woman in the center of the room, as she clears her throat.

It's story time.

***

Act 4

I was four years old when I wrote my first bit of prose. This was long before I realized my passion for poetry. It was some silly thing about a crab who crossed paths with a seagull. I wish I'd kept it. I, I showed it to my mother, she read it and said, and I never forgot this: 'It's a cute story, Celeste, but the crab shouldn't forgive the seagull so quickly for taking its food.' My first bit of constructive criticism. I changed the ending, deciding the crab and seagull should not just kiss and make up. But it made me sad... Mother liked it much better, and I was too young to realize the lesson therein – that forgiveness must be earned. That sometimes, no matter how hard you try to get it, it won't be given to you.

Some things you don't forgive, right?

Anyhow, as a child, and a rather timid one, I spent the majority of my time writing. Reading too, of course, but I found that I preferred the things I wrote to those that other people did. How narcissistic, is it not? Most writers you come across absolutely abhor their texts; they seem to think everyone else is far more talented than they are. But I was happy with my pieces – my poems, my short stories. I started working on my first novel when I was ten, not long after my father left. I saw the toll it took on my mother, my sister. Divorce was not as accepted then as it is now.

Clare – that would be Nicole's grandmother, boys – went from being the most popular girl in school to being the daughter of a cheating bastard. She bounced back, overtime; but I was never popular to begin with, so, things only got worse for me.

But as always, I found solace in my writing. I made a character out of every single person around me. My mother was the perfectionist home-fairy, who tried to keep up appearances during the day though she cried herself to sleep each night. My sister was the prom queen who sought comfort in the superficial things in life, because to dig deeper would mean to fall apart. Her high school sweetheart, who became her husband, was also a character; as was Mr. Betts, the hypochondriac who taught me Geography; beefy lunch-lady Clorinda provided comic relief… Everyone around me had story potential. They made for this rich, colorful cast that filled my pages. I told their tales as I perceived them, and it took me the longest time to realize one character was missing from it all.

"Who?" Thomas asks.

Celeste wipes the corner of her eye before it gets a chance to tear up.

Who do you think?

It wasn't till I had two hundred pages worth of material that I realized I'd never written myself into the story. I didn't even act as the narrator, first-person was never my thing. I racked my brain trying to figure out what role I could play. I didn't have meaningful interactions with anyone in school. I didn't react when my father left. Not a tear shed, not a word said. There's absolutely nothing worse than a personage without personality, don't you agree? Take Snow White. Tragedy befalls her time and again, yet she exhibits no sign of distress, bewilderment, anger. Anything.

I was thirteen when I realized I had no story worth telling.

Which happened around the time every character in my novel was eclipsed by a new lead; someone who barged into town like she owned the place. Oh, my sister detested her! Clare was settled in her position as the prettiest girl in school. But our humble eyes had never met a beauty like Cassandra Palmer's.

"Okay, I need to stop you there," Thomas says, raising his hand, "Grandma was *pretty*?"

"I'm also confused," Nicole says.

Celeste chuckles.

'Pretty' doesn't begin to cover it.

Cassandra had a face which would have been held to the highest regards in any era she happened to be born in. The ancient Egyptians would have crowned her Queen. The Mayans would have deemed her too fair to sacrifice. The Greeks would have launched a million ships in her rescue, not a measly thousand. Her features were so delicate you'd think Michelangelo himself had carved them. Her skin so white the sun bounced right off. Her lips so red, her hair an impenetrable black. She was, without a shadow of a doubt, the fairest in all the lands.

But make no mistake, she wasn't devoid of personality. In fact, she had more of that than any person I'd ever met. Still does.

I saw in her an exciting protagonist. There's something inherently compelling about a hero who parachutes into a new town, knowing nobody, predicted to be the underdog, but who turns it around in the snap of a finger. Cassandra was this novelty that never wore off. Beautiful, but smart. Cunning, yet charming. I, like everyone, was fascinated by her.

But nobody admired her like your grandfather.

Thomas' interest reaches a new peak. He can tell we're getting to the good stuff.

Not the adjective I would use, though.

Oh, Albert.

He was by no means what we in the day called a 'rubbernecker'; there was nothing delicate about his features. His hairline began receding before he even hit puberty! But he had this quirky, almost aloof quality to him that went unnoticed by all girls. All but one.

By the time I was fifteen, I realized I was in love with Albert Keane. Shortly after realizing he was in love with Cassandra. Who was head over heels for Ferdinand Plum. Oh, my heart goes to out to you kids these days, you'll entangle yourselves in these shallow romances and think each of them are life-or-death.

You don't know what life-or-death is.

But I digress. It was a story as timeless as they come, wasn't it? The true underdog revealed himself. The poor, hardened country boy in love with the ice princess. He had his work cut out for him, what with every boy in school longing for Cassandra's hand.

The biggest competition was her stepfather, but that's neither here nor there.

Thomas raises his hand again. "I'm sorry to interrupt but, if Grandma's father had also left, wouldn't she have been disgraced like your sister?"

Celeste gives him a solemn look. "Her father didn't leave, dear, he perished." She takes a pause. "Word got around that Alistair had killed him, in fact. Taken his place. Most people dismissed it as a vicious, unfounded rumor. Those of us who *knew* Alistair had reason to believe."

She breathes in.

But that's not the focus right now.

Albert was popular enough, had a nice circle of friends; Horace Towers, Ray Carson, they usually hung around together. I can see them now, by the apple tree that grew in our schoolyard.

Albert's family was remarkably poor. They had a bit of land that they used to sustain only themselves. I know Albert dreamed of becoming successful, rich even, by any means necessary. Preferably the quickest means, which is why, as you can probably guess, he devoted himself to contraband at such a young age.

But the fact is, back then his family could barely afford to send him to school, let alone pay for his supplies. Horace always shared his books with him. But one day – a Wednesday, I recall, God knows why I do – Horace was sick, and Mr. Betts asked Albert to sit with me. Wrong, he asked *me* to sit with Albert, at the front of the class. Walking from the very last row up to his desk, right before the blackboard, felt like walking the green mile. I could sense all eyes on me, and I remember thinking I might faint. But the worst bit was when I reached my destination, and this dopey, bubbly country boy I had admired for more than a year gave me his hand and said, 'Hey, I'm Albert. Are you new?'

The children let out a collective, "Ouch!" But Celeste lets herself laugh.

I was so mortified I told him yes.
That I was Celeste Colm, fresh from Aroncho, new to school. It was years before he learned the truth and we both laughed about it. Anyway, Albert was the kind of guy who never forgot those who were nice to him, so he kept talking to me. Greeted me as we crossed one another in the hall. Sat with me at lunch sometimes, introduced me to his friends. Told me all about his home, his parents, his dreams. And his love.

His grandiose, transcending, effervescent love for the prettiest girl in school. He always joked about it, him having no chance, but I could hear the sorrow in his voice, behind the jokes. Cassandra represented an innate fear of his, that he would never amount to anything. She was the treasure at the end of the rainbow, always so near, always out of reach.

Through Clare, I met Glory. Once my sister's best friend, then Cassandra's. In my novel, I described Glory Gardner as a windmill, turning in whichever direction the draught blew. But Glory was the key to Cassandra. She knew everything about everyone in school, everyone who mattered anyway, and she introduced us both, after briefing me on her. I told Cassandra I needed to write a fluff piece for the school paper and decided to focus on the prospected prom queen. She thought it would be great for her campaign.

Thomas smiles, delighted by the story, even if the characters in it don't seem to correspond to their names. His grandmother, a beautiful prom queen? It had to be fiction.
"Did she win?" Nicole wonders.
Celeste lowers her head.
"No, fate had other plans for her."

Much crueler ones.
Cassandra and I got closer than I could have anticipated. I don't believe she was particularly enthralled by my company, but she saw in me a sincerity that escaped most kids around her. She once told me she felt lonely all the time, at every pep rally, every debate. People always wanted to know what Cassandra was thinking, yet she felt like no one listened to her. Only I did.
So, she confided in me. I got to know how much she adored her late father. Resented her mother. Feared her stepfather. And how adorably obsessed she was with Ferdinand, the only guy who played hard to get around her. She said he reminded her of David Cassidy. Oh, you kids wouldn't know who that is!

"Star of *The Partridge Family*," Thomas says, "half-brother of Shaun Cassidy, sang 'Daydreamer', amongst other hits."
Celeste smiles. "I'm impressed."

"My Godpa's obsessed with number-one songs," he adds, "you hang around him long enough, you learn a thing or two."

Nicole chuckles unwillingly.

Well, back to Albert and Cassandra.

The first time I mentioned him to her, she twitched her nose, no idea whom I was speaking of. I made sure to talk him up as often as possible, get her accustomed to the name. And everything Cassandra told me, in strictest confidence, was then shared with Albert. I knew it was wrong, but I got the strangest fulfilment out of my role as cupid in their love story. Like I was living it myself.

Every time Albert spoke of Cassandra, with such longing in his doe eyes, I smiled as though he were talking about me. But every time I spoke of him to Cassandra, I made sure not to denounce my feelings – if she knew how much I wanted him, she would probably show even less interest. Eventually, I introduced them, and they hit it off right away. Both constantly entertained by each other's sense of humor; Albert's was slaphappy and innocent, Cassandra's dry and morbid. I usually sat nearby and just listened to them trade verbal blows endlessly, and I could feel the sparks flying.

I was, yet again, a third-person narrator in a love story, enticing my characters to move the plot along. I told Glory she was all Ferdinand ever talked about; I told *him* Glory would have relations with every boy who took her out for dinner. Which would be shameless slandering on my part, were it not true.

With this, I set the stage for an important scene in our drama: the night of St. John's.

In 1976, the church collapsed. Which is an interesting story unto itself, one that delves into the supernatural, but we don't have time for that. The point is, St. John's party that year was moved to the bull ring. Albert had decided that'd be the night he'd take his shot at Cassandra, whereas she was there to dance with Ferdinand. But Glory was all over the latter, so Cassandra had to settle for your grandfather. It was delicious to watch.

I hadn't counted on the surprise appearance of a villain. Alistair barged in, like a raging colossus; he reduced Albert to a puddle – you don't wish to know what of – and dragged Cassandra out. It was for the best, in a sense; Cassandra admired the fact that Albert had come to her defense, and they finally became a couple. They dropped out of school and got married, shortly after she became pregnant with Margaret. Ferdinand married Albert's sister – your aunt Doris, Thomas – which caused many grievances for all involved, but again, neither here nor there. Glory was paired off with poor Cyril, even though he was clearly – well, doesn't matter.

And I was alone, still. With an unfinished story.

I moved to Hovel Street, across from the newly married Keanes. Which didn't help one bit with the fact that I was still in love with Albert. I visited nearly every day, helped raise their children, pried on their problems, and found creative ways to solve them. And boy, did they have problems... Albert's stint in jail, the affairs they both led, every day was a drama with them. It didn't hit me till I'd turned forty that I had never lived my own life, as I was too busy living theirs. Feeling this sad satisfaction every time their marriage was on the rocks.

In the mid-nineties, they hit another one of their rough patches, about Albert's increasing problem with alcohol. Well, it was just during one of the many afternoons he spent at Mr. Arnold's that I ran into him, and we got to talking. It felt like we were back in high school, confiding in one another, only instead of telling me his dreams and aspirations, he told me about his problems with the wife and kids. He told me he felt stuck in a never-ending night. That no matter how much he waited it out, or moved forward, the sun would never rise. He kept waiting for something, someone, to shine a little light on him.

"So, *you* did," says Thomas. "That's why he says he could have had sunlight with you. But he chose the night."

Celeste closes her eyes and inhales, clutching the letter over her lap.

Thomas continues. "He also said he could never tell you something. What was it?"

Celeste really doesn't want to answer. It pains her to admit it. But she does. "That he loved me. I said I loved him all the time. He could never say it back."

"Why not?" Alfie asks.

Celeste looks up at him. "Because he didn't. I was but a distraction for Albert, a means of escaping his wretched life. I didn't mean anything to him."

Nicole shakes her head, causing some tears to come out. "He thought he was going to die, and his last instinct was to write to you. You must have meant something."

Celeste gives her a hint of a smile.

Perhaps I did.

Monastery   *Renato Belindro*

That day, at the bar, out of commiseration, I leaned in to give Albert a comforting peck on the cheek, but – he grabbed my face and kissed me. On the lips.

I do hate clichés, but it truly felt like I'd died and gone to heaven. My every schoolgirl fantasy came true that very moment. We tried to keep some distance between us after that incident, but over time we found ourselves caught in an affair. Right across the street from Cassandra. We would write each other letters, agreeing to meet up. We left them in my mailbox, since his was not an option.

There was a rush that came with it all, one no words can't describe. All of my senses were perfectly aware of how immoral it was, and none of them seemed to care. I rationalized things to a point where I blamed Cassandra for my own wrongdoing, telling myself that if she were a better wife, he wouldn't cheat on her. Somehow, I blocked out all the other mistresses Albert had before me, and at the same time as me.

Being with him was the most alive I had ever felt.

Nicole feels herself getting hot under the collar as she swallows dry. Keep it cool, sweetheart.

"We kept the affair going for years, Cassandra being none the wiser. Oh, she knew Albert was an adulterer, and she'd caught many of his lovers and made them pay. But me, her best and only friend? Not a chance in hell. Until, well, something happened that made our affair no longer imperceptible."

"He got you pregnant," Thomas guesses.

Celeste doesn't answer.

"W-What?" Nicole can't process this right away.

"That DNA test we found," Thomas says, "the one with the positive maternity results. He had you tested, didn't he?"

Nicole is on alert mode. "Who?!"

Celeste nods sedately. "I didn't know he would do that. I figured it was the sort of thing you needed my consent for, but apparently Francis knows someone at the hospital lab."

"WHAT?" Nicole brings up her hands, her chest heaving without her realizing it. "Wait. No, wait, I – you have a son? And it's *Francis*?!"

"Honey, I –"

"Francis is my cousin?!"

Nicole might not be able to assimilate this yet, but Thomas' head, always faster than everyone else's, takes it to the next level: David and Fred are related to Francis; Francis is related to Celeste; Celeste is related to Nicole. So, Nicole –

Oh, boy.

Celeste sighs. "Back to our story."

The three kids assume their positions, still reeling from the news.

Albert got me pregnant.

When Cassandra found out – well, no point in getting into that. The story ended with Francis living with them. It felt like a just punishment, which is what made me realize my mother had a point with the crab and seagull story – that some things you don't forgive. Me losing my child to them was payback for all I'd done to that family.

For years, Francis and I weren't allowed to have a relationship. He was lied to, told Cassandra was his mother, and I a simple neighbor. After Albert's passing, however, we began spending time together, sometimes with Cassandra's permission. I think she felt like she'd painted herself into a corner when she took him in. It was an apt punishment for me and Albert, but once he was gone, it was just a burden she could no longer shake off. So, I helped lighten the load by looking after him most days. She even took to coming around, showing me what few pictures and mementos she'd kept of his early days. I – I think deep down she wanted some company.

I told Francis all about his father, with whom he had never been close. That included everything about the 'treasure' Albert left behind.

Celeste actually did quotation marks with her fingers when she said 'treasure' – bless her. The kids' interest reaches yet another peak when they were sure the story couldn't get better.

"You know about the money?" Nicole asks.

"Of course she does," Thomas says, "why else would Grandpa have brought it up in his last letter?"

"He didn't just tell me," Celeste says with a smile, "he showed me. In a manner of speaking. Your grandfather, well, he became involved in some obscure dealings late in his career as a smuggler. Ironically, when free circulation became a thing, border patrol tightened. Contraband was a far more dangerous venture, and much less lucrative. To make up for that, Albert found himself entangled with a drug cartel."

"With someone called Mad Dog," Thomas says.

"How do you know that?"

"I did my research," he says, proudly.

Yes, well.

One afternoon, in the early noughties, Albert showed up at my door in a panic. The police were fast on his trail, and the money was all the evidence they needed to connect him to their investigation on the cartel. He asked if he could keep it with me for a while, and I agreed. As always, I would have done anything for that man. So, he brought in the chest he had made – a large, metal box from some place called 'Chubby Chester', which I found amusing. I kept it in my attic until he was in the clear and able to move it. I asked where he would take it, and he didn't want to say. But he gave me something.

Nicole, dear, would you reach in that drawer there and fish out my agenda?

Nicole obliges. She gets up, opens the drawer of a bureau, takes out the agenda and hands it to her aunt, who opens it in the middle and takes out a square of paper. She unfolds it before the kids' watchful eyes, and Thomas' jaw takes a freefall.

77-04-09.

Again.

My grandson almost jumps at her. "What is that?! Tell me, tell me now!"

"Easy," Nicole says as she pulls him back.

The truth is, I don't know.

I asked him what it meant when he handed it over, and he said, "If anything happens to me, the money can stay with whoever finds it first. If you really love me, if you really *know* me, and my history, this code is all you need to find it."

He kissed me on the forehead and left, to hide the money elsewhere. To this day, I don't know what he meant by that. I thought I knew Albert, and his story – hell, I wrote down most of it. But I can't for the life of me find out where he kept his money, or what these numbers mean.

But I thought, maybe Francis could figure it out? I told him everything about the chest and the code, hoping to instill in him some interest in his father's life. If he found the money, it would more than make up for the life of neglect he'd had so far. Albert would have wanted him to find it, I'm sure.

I'll be honest, I never thought much about who should have the money. It might be the omniscient in me – I *know* who's getting it in the end, so I never considered other possibilities.

"So, we were right," Thomas says, "Francis has been looking for Grandpa's money all along."

"That's why he dug all those holes at the Old Farm," Nicole says, "and had the code and all that stuff about his father at Beresford."

"I gave him the keys to the manor, and the garage," Celeste says, "I thought he could use a base of operations, if you will. Somewhere no one would intrude. I should have known you kids would be too sharp to get away from."

Okay, knock it off, Thomas – if you keep grinning like that, your face might get stuck that way.

"Okay, so you told him about his father," Alfie says, "but how did he learn you were his mom?"

Celeste almost flushes, feeling suddenly foolish.

Why, over fava beans, if you can believe that.

It was just last year that it happened. Francis came over for lunch, and I made him sautéed fava beans with toasted bread, one of his favorite things in the world. He was eating them with such gusto and commenting on how sad it was that nobody else at home liked favas – especially Cassandra, who abhorred them. I was toasting more bread as he ate, and he asked me, "Did my father like these?"

"God, no," I said, "he couldn't stand the sight of them."

He frowned and said, "Well, I like them."

To which I absent-mindedly responded, "Of course you do, you're your mother's son."

Then I froze.

He was staring at me inquisitively, wondering what I'd meant by that. We had just talked about Cassandra hating fava beans.

I don't know what it was. A mere slip of the tongue, or the more Freudian kind. Perhaps I was subconsciously speaking my truth, or sabotaging our relationship, as I have most relationships in my life. I can't be sure. But it happened.

That was the extent of our discussion on the matter. I'm sure, however, he had that in the back of his mind for a while, eating away at him – possibly connecting dots he hadn't before, questioning certain beats in his life. After he took that DNA test, apparently from stealing my toothbrush, we had an enormous argument I don't wish to replay. I found myself losing him all over again.

Until he came around one afternoon. And I could tell it wasn't for fava beans.

He had this malicious smirk I'd never before seen on his face. As if he knew he was about to do something wrong and looked forward to it.

I was in the kitchen putting a kettle on the stove and he walked in without announcing himself. But I swear I felt the temperature drop when he did.

"I forgot you fancied yourself a poet." This he said as he put one of my works down on the table. The first poem I sent you kids.

I was blindsided. It took a moment for my senses to return to me. When they did, the first thing I said was that I was sorry, which he brushed off with a scoff. "Not a problem," he said, "I think it's cute."

Cute. I felt offended, though I wasn't sure why. What did he think was 'cute'? My poetry? My trying to help you boys? Whatever the case, 'cute' sounded disparaging. Like he was mocking me.

"Just out of curiosity," he said, "why did you do it?"

I was stumped. The truth is, I didn't know. To this day I'm not sure why I felt the need to reach out to you kids. But the moment Cassandra told me what her grandsons were up to, I felt this unexplainable urge to help. I –

I think on some level I wanted her carted off to jail. I thought – maybe, just maybe, if she were out of the picture, Francis and I would stand a chance. That we could make up for lost time.

I realize how awful that is, Cassandra has other children. Even Fred and Henry live – well, only Henry now. Depriving them of their matriarch for my own gain was deeply selfish. If not unjust.

But the fact is, Francis had learnt the truth about the letters. Apparently, he had gotten the prints from his sister, Margaret.

"Wait!" Thomas puts up his hand, "Aunt Maggie *knows?*"

Indeed. Way to bury the lead, Celeste.

She nods. "I think the adults in your family have all known for some time, Thomas."

"Why didn't they say something, do something?" he asks.

"They have," she tells him.

Thomas' eyes blow up. "Rocky."

Celeste confirms this with her own eyes.

I was about to get to that.

I hoped to move Francis by explaining why I did what I did. That I always had him in mind, that I wanted a chance to be his mother. Additionally, impersonating Albert, morbid though it may be, felt like reuniting with him. As though he was whispering those words to me himself.

No comment.

Francis wasn't moved, however.

As it turns out, he hadn't come for an explanation. He had come with an agenda.

"I need you to write me another letter, just like the others," he said, before asking where I kept my stationery.

I was confused, and curious. I pointed in the direction of the living room desk and as he reached for the materials, he told me his mother – he always calls her 'my mother' – had wanted to come in his place, settle the score with me, but he had volunteered himself, to help keep the peace.

He put the paper and pen down on the kitchen table and pulled the chair for me. Then he said I just needed to write down what he dictated.

Which I began to. But the moment he finished saying, 'If you want to see your dog alive again', I dropped the pen. I was struck by a numbing fear. I asked what he meant by that, what he intended to do.

"You leave that to me," he said. I felt my throat sink into my stomach. What was he getting me into?

I told him I didn't feel comfortable. That I wouldn't go on unless he told me exactly what his plan was, whether he wanted to harm Rocky. He refused to tell me, and I refused to do it. So, he – he –

"Aunt Cel?"

Deep breaths, come on. You can do this, Celeste. It's not even the worst bit of the story. Far from it.

"What did he do?" Thomas asks.

Celeste grips her wrist lightly. It's gone from purple to black, and the mere graze of her fingertips makes it hurt.

Well, you all know the letter was sent.

I tried to get up from the chair, but he pushed me down by the shoulders. For the first time in more than twenty years, someone reduced me to nothing again. I never expected it to be my own son.

He picked up the pen and put it in my hand, closing my grip around it. "Just write down what I tell you," he ordered.

I screamed no, which isn't like me. I rarely shout; Nicole, dear, you know that's true. I tried to get up again and he, he grabbed my wrist a-and twisted it. I screamed in pain, and he pushed me down again, slammed my arm on the table so hard that the pen exploded in my hand. He yelled, "Write it!", right in my ear and I-I began to cry. He ignored it. He went to grab another pen as I sobbed at that table and he – he said he wouldn't leave until I'd done it.

So, I did it. I could barely see from the tears, my wrist ached horrors, but I wrote everything he told me, doing my best to replicate Albert's calligraphy. When h-he got to the part of sending 'attached evidence', I feared the worst. I knew he would hurt Rocky. I-I wanted to tell you the whole truth, everything I knew, but I was afraid.

Afraid he'd hurt *me*.

Nicole grabs her aunt's wrist. "Son of a bitch."

Hey. Lest you forget, the bitch is your aunt.

"So," Thomas says, "they are all in on it. Francis, Grandma, Aunt Maggie. They know what we have been doing all along, and they took Rocky to try and stop us."

Celeste wipes her tears. "I couldn't say."

"Well, can you say who killed our grandfather?"

Celeste shakes her head.

"Please," Thomas says. "You must know something. You said my grandmother started coming by after his death. Did you ever notice anything unusual?"

Celeste's reluctance to answer is more telling than she intended.

"She killed him," Thomas says, "didn't she?"

Celeste looks down.

I can only assume so.

I never forgot that day. June 23rd, 2005. It was about five in the afternoon, and I was making chocolate-chip cookies when Cassandra came over. Francis loved them, so I always gave him some on the sly, under the condition that he not tell his moth- Cassandra.

But that day, things changed.

I had just put them in the oven when I heard a frantic knocking. When I opened the door, Cassandra looked – I can't even describe it. She seemed lost, above anything else. I barely took notice of it, but she was wearing her large, brown cardigan, which she only wore in the winter. She told me, and I quote, "Francis comes back at a quarter to six. I need you to look after him for the night. Pick him up at the bus stop, don't let him go home no matter what."

My chin nearly fell to my feet. I had never been allowed to have a relationship with Francis before then; what little time with him I could steal for myself was always short-lived because of her. But there she was, telling me to take him in, to care for him. Even if just for the night, it meant everything to me.

I asked her why and nearly kicked myself for that. Why ask? Why not just run with it, be glad for it?

She validated these thoughts, when she said, "What do you care? He's yours for the night."

Then she turned to walk away, but me being the idiot I am, I had to ask if everything was alright. She turned to me, did this strange gesture with her fist, almost like she was clenching it in rage, and told me, in a passive-aggressive voice, "Celeste, I'm having a bit of a day here."

When her hand went back down, my eyes followed it.

That's when I saw the blood. The thinnest stream, emerging from the cardigan, drying on her leg.

I looked back at her, her face, and noticed little droplets on the collar of her blouse. She was covered in blood. I could only imagine what she looked like underneath the cardigan.

I think she realized I had noticed but didn't say anything. She'd done what she'd come here to do, it was up to me to follow the simple directives. Keep Francis occupied for the day. So much more than I had ever hoped for.

The following day, Nana Beth went around town to inform everyone of Albert's passing the night before, from a stroke. Asking people to be respectful of the family, not to ask any questions in this difficult time.

I didn't cry.

I didn't gasp, blink, emote in any way. Something inside had told me, all through the night, my Albert had died. At her hands.

After a while, my numbness turned to relief, when I realized why I hadn't felt sad. It wasn't just that I knew she'd killed him. It was that I knew Albert was better off. I could feel it.

He was dead long before that June afternoon. But on that day, he got to live again.

I know he did.

Well. I don't know about you, but I've got something in my eye. Apparently, I'm not the only one either. Alfie and Nicole find themselves wiping their own tears, same as Celeste. But Thomas? Touched though he may be – and he isn't unaffected, I can assure you – he's more confused than anything else.

"Miss Colm," he says, "I sympathize with what you've gone through, and applaud you for your courage in coming clean, as well as for doing it so eloquently. But it appears you have skipped an important chapter of your story."

Celeste looks down from him, like she can guess what he's getting at.

"We have the 'before' and 'after' of Francis coming into the world as your biological son. But please explain to us how it is that my grandmother, who is far from a nurturing individual, came to pose as his mother?"

Celeste forces a smile through her new bout of tears. Her hands tremble on her lap, and a small sob clumps up in her throat.

"She took him to replace her own child, didn't she?" Thomas suggests, "She somehow got the real Francis killed and used your son to replace him."

Celeste's head jerks in confusion. "What?"

"No need to deny it, we found blood on the crib, and on a toy car! We know a child died in that house. Francis was his replacement, correct?"

"I don't know what you're saying," Celeste tells him. "There's only one Francis. There's only ever been one."

"Then what happened?" Nicole asks. "Whose blood did we find?

Sigh. Here it is.

With some strain, Celeste pushes down whatever keeps clogging up her throat.

On to the next chapter.

***

Act 5

I'm afraid I must take over from here. Celeste made for a compelling narrator and an interesting change, but this part of her story hits too close to home. She will tell it to the kids, sure, well enough that they get the gist of it. But I want you to have a clear picture – and there's no room for filters.

Francis, the one and only, was born on March 19th, 1998. Spring was nearly in full swing, and Celeste sat in her favorite alcove at Beresford Lot that morning, looking out the window. The almonds were in bloom, their flowers like snow on the treetops. She thought back to the one time it had snowed in Monastery, that harsh winter of 1976, shortly before the church collapsed.

Celeste felt an odd tightening in her stomach and clutched it. That's when her waters broke all over the pillows, catching her completely off-guard – she wasn't due for another two weeks. It seemed her baby boy was more than enthusiastic to come into the world. From a current, more informed perspective, he should have known better.

Celeste rushed to the phone and powered through her first contractions. "Nana! Nana, it's time, my – *argh* – my waters broke! Please come! Yes, Beresford!"

She didn't put the phone away once the call was ended. Someone else had to be contacted. Try to guess who.

Afterwards, Celeste followed Nana's advice and lied down in her guest bedroom downstairs. She was glad to still be wearing her nightgown, which ought to facilitate matters.

About half an hour later, when the afflictions in her stomach were roughly ten minutes apart, Celeste heard the front door open. "Here, Nana!" she called. "In the guest room!"

Another spasm, making her coil up and close her eyes. She wanted to scream, but the pain didn't allow for that. When she opened her eyes, the sight of Cassandra at the door was more gut-wrenching than the contractions.

"Cas– Cass–" Celeste well tried, but her short breath, mixed with a newfound, staggering horror, kept the words from coming out.

Cassandra shushed her as she moved in closer. "Don't strain yourself. How far apart are they?"

"What – where's Nana?"

"Something's detained her. I was there when you called, so I came instead."

Allow me to translate this: Cassandra pushed Nana Beth into the pantry and locked the door.

"How far apart?" my wife asked again.

"Um, uh, ten minutes?"

Cassandra nodded. "Alright. You're gonna have to suffer through them a bit longer, till they're three to four minutes from each other."

"W-Will Nana be here by then?"

"I don't think she can make it, Celeste. I'll help you myself."

"B-But you're not a midwife."

"I crapped out five kids already, I think I know the drill." She put her hand over her own protruding belly and said, "This one'll make six. Jesus, I really need to get my tubes tied."

Celeste puffed out, in a vain attempt to withstand the pain. Cassandra rubbed her friend's stomach and said, "On second thought, maybe it's Albert who needs to get snipped. What's the point of me making sure I have no more kids, if my husband's going around fertilizing his hookers?"

There it was. Celeste had opted to give her the benefit of the doubt – she wasn't in a position to do otherwise – but Cassandra's mean streak always burst out.

My wife's attention was diverted by something else. She put her purse down in the desk of the alcove – every room in the manor had one – and walked around the bed. She placed her hand on the railing of the pink crib, tucked against the corner of the room, and gritted her teeth.

"Albert told me he sold this." She laughed to herself, and my blood curdles as I hear it now. "He said, 'We're not having any more kids, honey, what the hell are we keeping it for?'" She turned back and grabbed her stomach again. "Ironic, huh?"

Celeste didn't know what to say.

"Can't believe it's been twenty-two years since we got this," my wife added. "It was one of the first things Albert smuggled in for us. For Margaret." She noticed the blue plush bunny inside the crib and picked it up. "Did Albert give you this? How sweet."

Celeste couldn't deal with her friend's more passive form of aggressiveness, not at that moment. "Cassandra, why are you here?"

"To help, of course. You're a backstabbing cow, and my husband a filthy manwhore, but none of that is the kid's fault."

Celeste breathed in, with trepidation in her eyes. Another contraction ensued.

"They're closer now, huh?"

My wife sat on the bed and put her hands over Celeste's knees, slowly parting her legs.

"Well, then. Let's pop out the little bastard."

Within the hour, the little bastard was born. Celeste had witnessed many a delivery, as Nana Beth's second-in-command, but it's one thing to watch, another to experience. In that moment, she feared she might never walk again – her legs refused to join, and the minimum movement sent a biting pain up her body. Her breath slowly returned to its normal rate, but the thumping headache that came with made her wish she were put down.

With what little strength she had, she pulled herself up and sat on the bed. Across the room, Cassandra gently rocked the newborn in her arms.

Celeste could see her child's head sticking out of the blanket he'd been wrapped in. Delicate as porcelain. Her heart nearly burst with a joyous warmth, the kind no amount of pain could undo. My own heart isn't unaffected, by the way; I'd forgotten about this, but Francis was a beautiful baby. His buxom cheeks were pink as cotton candy; his little ears carved like roses; his nose a cute button you just wanted to click.

I'm afraid I lied, without meaning to. I hadn't forgotten about any of that. I simply never took notice of it when I had a chance to.

Neither did Cassandra, even in that moment. She rested the child over her pregnant belly, yet she took in none of the traces of the beautiful face she'd cleaned herself.

Celeste's eyes welled up and she broke the calm that reigned in the room. "I-I don't know what to call him."

Cassandra rubbed the boy's head. "I like Francis."

"Francis?"

"It's what, um –" My wife felt a slight choke. "It's what I almost called my –"

She couldn't finish, but Celeste understood. As do I.

"I thought about it when Nate was born," Cassandra said, "but couldn't bring myself to do it."

Celeste rubbed her eyes. "It's a beautiful name. I-I think it means, 'free man'."

She took a deep breath before going further.

"I'm sorry. So sorry, Cassandra. I-I know that's not enough; it will never be. It won't undo the amount of hurt I've caused you. But God knows how sorry I am." Celeste brought the sheet to her eyes and wiped them, but the prickling persisted in them. "And I will do whatever it takes to make it right with you, to have my friend back."

Cassandra bit her lip. "I'm glad you say so."

The tears drizzled down Celeste's face, their saltiness stinging her reddened cheeks. "And, and I know nothing excuses what I did, so believe me, I don't mean to justify myself in any way, but I honestly believed that – that you and Albert were doomed."

She closed her eyes momentarily and breathed in. "That you could never be happy together. And I loved him, Cassandra." Her voice began to crack. "I always did, ever since high school. I resigned myself to thinking we could never be because I knew how much he adored you. But I've watched your marriage unravel over the last twenty years and I told myself that the two of you also couldn't be. When Albert – when he kissed me the first time, I became that foolish schoolgirl again. I thought – I told myself we'd all been cast in the wrong roles. That we were wasting our lives, but there was still time to reverse that! To find a way to – to just be happy."

Cassandra remained demure through this. Her eyes solely on the dormant baby.

Celeste leaned back and wiped her tears again, her face almost as sore as her legs. "But like I said, I was foolish. Nothing's changed. Long as he lives, Albert will love only one woman, no matter how many others he's with. I had to find that out the hard way."

Cassandra spoke at last. "He loves me?"

Celeste forced a smile. "With all his heart."

"Good," my wife said, "I'm glad."

Celeste sat forward again. "So now, I'll be left with him." She gestured at the baby. "I know this is hard, for all of us. But I can move away if it's easier for you."

"No. Stay."

"Really? You're sure?"

Cassandra nodded, still not looking at her.

Celeste joined her hands before her mouth. "God. Cassandra! You don't know what this means to me, I was so scared! Of everything, of what people would say, or how I'd raise a baby all by myself, whether Albert would acknowledge him, but I was especially afraid of *you*! How *you* would react. I – I almost terminated the pregnancy."

She felt a knot in her throat. As if it weren't enough how hoarse it got from all the shouting she did during labor. "But that day you saw me in the hospital, when I nearly lost the baby, I thought, it must be a sign from God that I didn't. He wanted me to know how it would truly feel. Because I swear, Cassandra, in that moment, I didn't care about anything, me, you, Albert, anyone but *him*!" Her eyes fell on her son again. "All that mattered was him. I never wanted to have a baby, but after I took that fall, I never wanted to be without him."

"You didn't fall, dear, I pushed you."

...

Celeste felt fainter than before – the air was sucked out of her, out of the room. She couldn't move, not her eyes, not her lips, not anything. It seemed the mattress had closed in around her hands, keeping her captive. The woman across the room, whom she'd known for decades, was a stranger. A dangerous stranger.

Who held Celeste's child in her arms.

Celeste's lips parted and did their job, however hesitantly. "W-What?"

Cassandra looked up from the baby, her face devoid of any perceivable emotion. "I snuck in and pushed you down the stairs. I wanted you to miscarry."

Celeste needed to breathe. Some way, somehow, the air had to get back in her lungs. But something kept blocking it. In fact, every organ in her body seemed on the verge of shutting down.

Cassandra lowered her head to face the newborn again. "I saw the gash on the floor, on my way in. The one made by your fall. Nasty thing." She paused. "I don't know what possessed me, Celeste, but I was so furious it felt like the only thing to do. I regretted it right away, when I saw you sprawling down those stairs, but by then it was too late. I rushed out and left you there, I – I thought you were dead. I thought, 'Well, crap. I just killed my only friend.' It wasn't like the other times. I felt awful. Guilty. And, unavenged. I didn't really know why."

Celeste finally moved, lifting the sheet off her. "Ca-Cassandra, I –"

Cassandra rocked the baby still, her eyes always on him. "When they called me from the hospital and said you'd survived the fall, I was so relieved. It was like God had given *both* of us a second chance. Francis, too."

Celeste put one foot on the floor, hoisting herself up. Her legs felt like they'd been broken apart by clamps and could crumble at any point. "Cassandra, can, can I hold my baby? Please?"

You could hear the despair in her voice. My wife looked up from the child, shook her head and mouthed a simple, 'No.' Then looked down again.

"Just, put yourself in my shoes," Cassandra said. "After everything I've been through, that I told *you* about –" The tears began to creep up, but Cassandra rammed them back down through sheer will. "I didn't deserve this. I *don't* deserve this."

"I know!" Celeste managed to stand. "Cassandra, I know, I –"

"I kept thinking what my life would be like the moment you gave birth. You, parading your love child up and down the street. Me, cooking dinner for him on the odd weekend, pretending not to hate his guts. Everyone in town laughing behind my back, and Albert, *Albert*! Sinking deeper into your pit. Having all the more reason to go and see you, spend time with you. Pull away from me."

The self-willing wasn't working anymore – the tears flowed out of Cassandra's mean little eyes, some falling on my son's face.

But her tears were no match for Celeste's. "Cassandra, please!" She reached out her arms and dared to step closer, albeit slowly. "Please, give me my baby!"

"It wouldn't be fair. Seeing you and my husband's kid every day, getting a constant reminder of your disgusting betrayal. No! No, I don't deserve to be punished like that, I wouldn't have it, never, but then – then I thought –"

She looked up, and her eyes pierced through Celeste's soul.

"I thought, that would be so fitting *for you*."

The chill that coursed through my mistress proved more searing than her labor pains. Almost lethal.

"Imagine it," Cassandra said, "you looking over *my* fence, seeing *your* kid in my front yard, day after day. Sleeping under my roof, eating my food, *loving me*. Like only a little boy can love his mother."

Celeste's head trembled. "No."

While Cassandra nodded hers. "I mean, could anything be more appropriate? You tried to destroy my family. So, I should only take yours."

"No!" Celeste wailed. "This, this is insane, Cassandra, you – you're pregnant too!" Celeste pointed at her friend's stomach. "Albert would never leave your kid for mine, never!"

Cassandra put the child down on the cushioned seat of the alcove and stood up.

"Please, y-you have nothing to worry about, I'll go away with him, you'll never see us again! You can't take care of your baby and mine, you –"

The words were pummeled out of her when Cassandra rolled up her blouse. And revealed the pregnancy pad underneath. The kind you try on maternity clothes with.

It was uncanny. Celeste found herself in a story the likes of which she couldn't have come up with. With an ending in sight that promised to be anything but happy.

Cassandra's smile contrasted with her tear-stained face. "It's incredible, what you can buy across the border." She undid the Velcro ligaments of the pad and plucked it from her torso. "Had to get them in all sizes, right after my sister-in-law told me you were knocked up. I mean, honestly, Celeste, you tried to keep that from me, but you got your first sonogram in Portalegrum? That vile tramp couldn't call me fast enough after you left."

Celeste tried desperately to take in all that had been thrown at her, but she couldn't grasp any of it.

Meanwhile, Cassandra laughed, almost maniacally. "God, Albert is such a *moron!* You have no idea how hard it was to keep this stupid fake gut from my kids, from our neighbors! I wanted to cut off Glory's fat hands every time she tried to rub my stomach. But Albert? He never even came near me, the asshole."

"You – you were faking –"

"Are you just catching up? If I wanted to take your damn kid, I couldn't just show up with him one day! People had to think I had one of my own coming."

Celeste brought her hands to her temples, completely overwhelmed. But she found it in her to speak, even if she sounded numb. "You're demented."

"I'm a scorned woman. You know what they say about us."

"You went to all this trouble just to punish me?"

"Pushing you down the stairs didn't cut it. Something was missing. But now, well, I may be reminded of what you did to me every day, but so will you. And knowing what it does to you will more than make up for me having to put the little bastard through school."

Celeste broke out of her stupor. "I don't know how you thought you'd make this happen, Cassandra, but it's an idiotic plan!"

My wife reached for her purse and opened it.

"If you think I'd ever let you take my baby, then you have to be out of your damn –"

The coherence that had made its way back to Celeste was siphoned out of her when Cassandra took out my revolver.

Which she lowered to point at my son's face.

"It's not really up for discussion."

Celeste paralyzed from head to toe, her eyes stuck on the harrowing sight before her, yet unable to see. And me? I see everything, clear as rain, but I still can't believe my own eyes, after twenty-one years.

I could have a million afterlives and never make sense of this.

"You don't get the picture, Celeste. The moment the cops come kicking down my door, they'll get the kid out in a body bag. If you try to take him in the still of the night, I will hunt you down – I mean, God, you tried to hide out here and I found you, I will always find you." She smiled again. "When I do, the kid's a goner. Make no mistake, I'd rather spend the rest of my days in jail than let you have him. I will blow him to kingdom come if I have to. But you? Oh, honey, you'll live to tell the tale, that's a promise. You like telling stories, don't you?"

Celeste's face swelled up like she was allergic to her own tears. She put one foot forward, instinctively, arms still reaching, all the while knowing it was hopeless.

"Believe me when I say you wanna stay where you are," Cassandra warned.

"P-P-Please!"

My wife reveled in her own maleficence. That, right there, was the bee's knees. No guilt, no regrets, only a deep sense of fulfilment – the kind that comes when justice is served.

Her joy was interrupted by the ebb and flow of the gun in her hand. She looked down to find little Francis, eyes closed, sucking on the muzzle.

Cassandra chuckled. "Aw, isn't that precious? He's probably hungry."

She sat back down and placed the revolver on her lap, then grabbed the baby while Celeste trembled in front of them. Then, she lowered her blouse and held the sleeping child to her breast.

Celeste couldn't move again, and I lack the words to explain what was happening to her in this moment. Cassandra peered at her blank face and grinned, reveling in her rival's hopelessness.

"See, you don't have to worry about a thing. I'm gonna be great to this kid, love him like he is my own."

Celeste teetered on the brink of passing out, as the baby's sucking noises rung in her ears. "No –"

"He's never gonna want or need for anything, Celeste."

"No, you, you can't –"

At that moment, the front door to the mansion opened. Cassandra put the baby down, covered herself, grabbed the gun again and pointed it at the door to the room.

You can imagine their surprise – and mine – when I showed my face. I expected to find my mistress in bed, our son in her arms. Instead, I found my wife holding me at gunpoint. With a flat stomach, no less.

"What – Cassandra?"

I wasn't much with words back then. But who would be, in a situation like this?

"What are you doing here?" I could feel the rage in my wife's voice. "You were supposed to be in the city!"

"Albert! Albert, please, she's insane!!"

"What are you doing here?!"

"I called him!" Celeste revealed.

Cassandra's eyes stayed on me. "Why?"

I held my hands up as though the police had caught me crossing the border. "Cassandra. Cassandra, honey, what are you doing?"

My heart had been on edge from the moment Celeste called me. It had raced faster than my car on the way back from the city. In that moment, it was on the verge of shooting through my chest.

"You weren't supposed to be here!" Cassandra cried, literally, with seething fury. "You ruined everything, you worthless drunk!"

I teared up and had no idea what about. "Cassandra, honey, I –"

I was interrupted by the baby's cries. Either from the loud noises or the fruitless attempt at feeding, I suppose. It marked the first time my eyes laid on him, and I felt more dumbstruck than I ever thought was possible.

Then I saw the pregnancy pad. I was never a quick thinker, but my mind raced with the most illogical conclusions. Which happened to be the right ones.

I forced myself to calm down. This wasn't the first extreme tantrum I'd witnessed from my wife, only the first involving a lethal weapon.

"Cassandra, just, please tell me what's going on."

"She's crazy!" Celeste screamed.

My eyes stayed locked with my spouse's. "Honey?"

Her lips trembled. "I *know*, Albert. I know you have an affair with her. I know about the kid."

The kid. My son, right there by the window. "Is that him?"

She nodded, and a tear slipped out.

"What about *our* kid?" I asked.

"There isn't one. I faked the pregnancy, so I could take hers and tell people it's mine."

I nodded in understanding. There was a simple logic to her lunacy. I couldn't comprehend why she would do something like that, but I could at least follow her plan.

"Alright. Okay, let's, let's calm down. Honey, I want you to stop and think about what you're doing."

"I have."

"That is Celeste's baby. You can't just take him; he doesn't belong to you."

"*You* belong to me. Yet she tried to take you."

I wanted to say that wasn't the same thing but feared it might fuel her wrath. "Okay, okay, Cassandra, tell you what, let's go home and talk about this." My arms hurt from staying up so long. "I have a lot to make up to you, we both do. But this isn't the way, it's – honey, this is –"

She rolled her eyes. "It's insane! Yes, Albert, I know!"

I nodded again. "You do."

"Of course I do, what am I, a moron? You think I don't realize how wrong this all is? How macabre?"

"Then, why are you doing it?"

Her bloated cheeks rose over the grin on her lips, further highlighting the wicked gleam of her eyes.

"Because I *want to*."

An unsettling iciness spread through me, numbing the pain in my arms. I could tell there was no insanity there. Just cold, calculated perversity.

"Albert, please, help me!" Celeste pleaded.

Bad move. My wife closed her eyes and breathed in, infuriated by my mistress addressing me. "Albert, dear, I think you should take the baby and go."

"What?" I spoke.

"I'm not crazy, but having you two in the same room might push me towards that. And I'm holding a gun, you don't *want* me to get crazy."

"No!" Celeste bellowed, "Please, no!"

Cassandra turned and pointed the gun at her. "Shut up! Shut your whore mouth! Haven't you done enough?!"

"You can't do this, you can't take my baby!!"

"Cassandra," I tried, "I can't do this."

"Albert!" She didn't look at me when she shouted. "I mean it! I'm this close to pumping her full of holes, you don't want that to be the first thing that child sees!"

I looked into Celeste's horror-struck eyes and knew mine showed even more fear.

"So, be a gentleman," Cassandra said, finally turning my way, "save your whore's life."

I paused. Looking back, this would have been one of those moments where you find yourself at a crossroads, and whatever decision you make will have terrible consequences. Would I side with the woman I exchanged vows with, for better or worse, or the woman who had, for years now, been the only thing capable of putting a smile on my face?

Neither.

I sided with *him*.

I moved slowly, carefully, towards the alcove and picked up my son. He began fussing and I shushed him, whispering lies that everything would be alright, as I walked out of the house with him in my arms. I closed the door behind me and got in the car.

From that day, Francis became mine and Cassandra's son. The Aroncho paper would announce his birth the following week. Nana would be told Celeste delivered a stillborn. I think deep down she always had her doubts but chose not to question it.

Even now, most of my children believe Francis to be their flesh and blood. Though Maggie eventually learned the truth – it seemed only fair for Cassandra to tell her she wasn't alone.

As for Celeste, the next time I saw her, she was a broken shell of the woman she used to be, and I mean that quite literally. I never asked her what happened after I left; I didn't want to know.

But you do, I'm sure. You didn't make it this far to not find out. And it's time I faced it myself.

Call it my punishment.

"Cassandra…"

On some level, I'm sure Celeste knew it was pointless – she had to have known. She could have begged on her knees, pleaded with joined hands, kissed Cassandra's feet, and it wouldn't have made a lick of difference. My wife was unwavering, unrepentant, and titillated.

"Please. Y-You can do whatever you want to me, beat me up, torture me, just don't take my baby!"

Cassandra grasped the gun so firmly, so steadily, you'd think she was a professional. "Remember Valerie?"

"W-What?"

She stepped closer. "I know you do. You remember the number I did on her, right?"

"Cassandra." Celeste, in turn, stepped backwards, around the bed, hands up.

"Or Della. Poor thing, she wasn't even sleeping with Albert. Didn't keep me from nearly turning her chin inside out."

Celeste wanted to wipe her tears, but she feared any movement might trigger Cassandra. The key word being 'trigger'.

"What are you saying?" she asked.

"You *know* what I'm saying! You were there with me through all that. Every damn time my husband tripped and fell into a slut, you helped me pick up the pieces, *their* pieces! You knew more than anyone how I handle betrayal, but you still did this."

Celeste's lips quivered. "Cassandra, p-please, I told you, I, I loved Albert, I – you can't help who you fall for. And he led me on!"

Cassandra nodded. "I'm sure he did. I'm sure he got a real kick out of doing it with my only friend. Cheating on me with nameless, faceless bimbos wasn't exciting enough, no, he had to *really* hurt me!"

Celeste's back pressed against the crib. Nowhere else to go from there.

"Thing is," Cassandra said, "Albert can do whatever the hell he wants to me, and he knows that. We're stuck together. I could end him just as good as he could end me, so we both just hang on for dear life, knowing all bets are off and anything goes. And I've hurt him more than he could ever hurt me." She looked proud of this. "He'll never be able to strike back as hard, believe that."

Celeste's terror mixed with an even more frightening bout of confusion. Where was she going with this?

"But you? I don't owe you s___! You knew there'd be hell to pay for this, Celeste. Be honest, your little story would be anticlimactic if there wasn't."

With a smile, she lowered the gun. Celeste was hit by a thin sensation of relief for the first in a while.

"I don't know why you did what you did," Cassandra said, "but you'll spend the rest of your life knowing why I did this."

She turned her back to leave.

Celeste watched her go as something arose in her. Then, "Because you deserved it."

The blood that ran hot in Cassandra's veins froze. "What?" she asked, not looking back.

"I didn't know why I did it either, for the longest time," Celeste said, almost as a whisper. "I felt so guilty, Cassandra. Like the worst person in the world. But now that I see this, see what you're capable of, I-I know why I did what I did. Why anyone ever hurts you. *You deserve it.* You deserve everything that comes your way."

The gun shook in Cassandra's trembling hand.

Celeste stepped closer, rubbing away her tears. "Albert cheating on you. Ferdinand not choosing you. Your mother, your stepfather. You're not the product of what other people do to you, Cassandra – you just bring out the worst in everyone. That's the kind of person you are."

She stood mere inches from my wife. "You say you're taking my son away because I deserve it. And I say I had sex with your husband for years, behind your back, under your own roof, because *you deserved it*."

THWACK!

Celeste nearly blacked out when the butt of the gun pounded her cheek. She fell onto the crib, her knees hitting the floor, her hair getting caught in the crevices of the railing. Cassandra walked towards her, grabbed her by said hair and –

THWACK!

"SAY THAT AGAIN!"

I couldn't hear Celeste's screams from the car. They deafen me now.

THWACK!

"SAY IT!"

The markings of the handle ripped Celeste's cheeks. Leading to scars that would never heal.

THWACK!

"TELL ME I DESERVED IT!"

Celeste's nose shattered, sending a thick scarlet stream down her chin. Which covered Cassandra's hand as she held her by the neck.

THWACK!

"COME ON NOW!"

The blood spattered all over the crib, the wall, the bunny. Celeste's front tooth broke off and slid down her throat, almost choking her.

THWACK!

"SAY IT AGAIN, YOU FILTHY –"

THWACK!

"WORTHLESS –"

THWACK!

"STUPID WHORE!!!"

Cassandra pushed her away and turned on her heels, catching her breath. Celeste, too, gasped for air, bringing her hand to her sore throat, her other hand nearly slipping on the reddened floor.

"By the way," Cassandra said, shaking the hand that had been covered in blood, "I'm gonna need the crib back."

She walked out at last.

We rode home in separate cars; me trying to hold the baby in place with one hand, her trying to keep from rear-ending me.

Wouldn't be long till Cassandra sent me for the crib. Which she took upon herself to scrub clean.

Evidently, she missed a spot.

***

Act 6

Since the investigation began, Thomas hasn't had much time to stop and think what the consequences would be, should he stumble upon the truth he yearned to find. Of course, he has yet to know who killed me – give it a few more hours – but he never fathomed what it would feel like when he got answers to questions he never thought he would ask.

Let me try and describe it: it feels like his stomach has turned into a washing machine doing a cycle, the shock, horror, and disgust all spinning inside, bumping into each other and into the walls of his body. As if that weren't enough, his head, too, is going for a spin. He stares at Celeste Colm in the chair across from him and can't even see her.

The other kids feel sick to their core as well. "Y-You said," Nicole tries, "you told me you got those scars in an accident."

I'm not sure if Celeste can hear her. Either way, she doesn't reply.

"Aunt Cel?" Nicole moves closer and grabs her arm.

Alfie can feel the tears trying to climb up his ducts; the pringling spreads to his nose and cheeks. What the hell has he gotten himself into?

When Thomas shakes his head, it's as if he's shaking off whatever turmoil was brought up in him. Out it goes. "Miss Colm, why – why did you let her do that?"

Celeste glances at him, unable to keep eye contact. "I deserved it," she muttered.

"No!" Nicole shakes her head, and her lips curl up. "Auntie, no."

"Miss Colm, I," Thomas says, "I can't begin to imagine what you've gone through. But," he gets up and kneels down in front of Celeste, holding her hand, "we can fix this. Francis isn't a baby anymore, we can go to the police, we –"

"How are you still friends with her?!" Nicole asks her aunt, cutting Thomas short. "She's always here, how – why do you let her?"

"I deserved it," Celeste answers.

"*She took your son!*"

Alfie feels the need to do something. "Nicole," is all he can say as he stands up and does nothing.

"She ruined your life!" Nicole screams, "She ruined *his* life! How can you – why did you –"

"I deserved it."

Nicole feels like her heart has been struck with a cattle prod. She reaches out to her aunt, sobbing uncontrollably, but brings her hand back to her mouth.

"Miss Colm," Thomas says, still on his knees, "please, try to think back on the poems you sent us."

"Thomas!" Nicole says.

"In the second one, you said something about lies, um, that four of my grandpa's children would remain demure –"

Nicole holds her aunt at last. "Thomas, drop it!"

Alfie grabs his friend's shoulder, but Thomas shrugs it loose. "– But the rest would join him in his cries. Who are they? Is one of them Francis? Who's the other one? What are the lies?"

"Thomas, knock it off!!" Nicole roars.

"Please!" Thomas grabs Celeste's hands tightly, to no effect.

"I deserved it," Celeste repeats.

That's all she'll say for a while. Thomas looks up at her eyes and sees a tiny light going out in them. Celeste retreats further and further into herself, where no one can reach.

"Miss Colm."

"Thomas!"

Alfie pulls at him. "Come on, leave her alone!"

"Miss Colm, please, I need to know!"

He grabs her apron and pulls at it, but it's no use. Celeste doesn't live there anymore. Nicole pushes him away with her foot and buries her sobbing head in her aunt's shoulder. Thomas gets up, with Alfie's assistance, and dusts himself off before heading out.

When he steps out through the door, everything that just happened comes back to him at once, and he throws up on Celeste's flowers.

The washer has finished its cycle.

Across the street, Cassandra walks out of her house to check the mail. She opens the green, house-shaped box and leafs through its contents: coupons, water bill, mortgage. Again.

She sighs. Yet another reminder of how deep in debt she is. Since Maggie didn't come through with a loan, the bank might foreclose the house, and with it goes the restaurant's collateral.

She closes the slot of the mailbox and prepares to head inside, but the sight of her grandson coming at her in a rapid pace confuses her. Thomas' hands are clenched, and his eyes shoot wrath. "You!" he calls.

"Thomas!" Alfie tries to stop him, but he could throw himself in front of his friend and I think Thomas would walk all over him. Cassandra rests the hand that's holding the mail over her waist and stands in wait.

"You know!" Thomas stops on the sidewalk before her. "You know what I have been up to, what all of us have been doing this summer. I know you do."

Cassandra bites the inside of her lower lip.

"I need you to understand one thing." If there was ever a moment to summarize how serious Thomas can be for someone his age, this would be it. "I embarked on this little project of mine driven by, first and foremost, curiosity. I wanted, nay, I *needed* to know what happened to my grandfather. The second motivator was the thrill of it all, the rush that came with doing something borderline dangerous. Third in line would be self-preservation. Should there be a killer in our family, we had a right to know, to protect ourselves."

Cassandra's lids lower ever so slowly, as if she's trying to focus on the image of him.

"But one thing it was never about, is justice. I did not entertain the thought of turning someone in my family over to the police, because I dreaded the notion. I just wanted to *know*. Upon learning the truth, I would figure out the best measure to handle it."

He steps closer. Alfie feels scared for his sake.

"Well. I dare say, I am inching closer and closer, and I already know how to handle it. Soon as I learn everything, soon as I am provided with every single bit of evidence on how it was all your fault, I am calling the cops on you."

The letters scrunch in Cassandra's hand.

"You know, before I learned the alphabet, the numbers, anything, I learned how to make excuses for you. Because that is what everyone needs to do in this family, turn the other cheek to your constant abuse. 'Grandma's been through so much.' 'Look what she has to deal with.'" He steps back. "No more excuses."

The rage bubbles up in my wife, nearly reaching her throat. I worry she might turn to a volcano should she open her mouth.

Thomas narrows his own eyes and breathes in as he looks up at her.

"Grandma... I am going to *destroy you*."

*

Inside the house, Henry starts sorting out his father's clothes for the week ahead. He usually does this on Sunday, but Fred's no longer around to iron them, so he must learn to do that first.

When he pulls a pair of work pants from the rack, he hears an odd jingling. He shakes them and hears it again. It's not coins, what on –?

He reaches into the pocket and takes out Rocky's red collar. With the little bell and the decorative bones.

When I tell you Henry stops cold, I mean it – his breath is sucked out of him so fast he might as well be dead.

At that same moment, Charlie teeters in, already tipsy. He's spent the last hour at Nate's warehouse, while his brother was away in the city. "Hengry?"

His son turns to him, holding the collar. "What is this?"

Charlie's reddened eyes widen. "Oops."

"Did you – where's Rocky?"

Charlie's look changes from one of 'busted' to one of annoyance. "Henry, Dad wanna take a nap, go out and play."

"Where is he?!"

"Don't yell at me." Charlie throws himself on the bed. "Daddy has a head hurt."

Henry grabs a handful of the clothes hanging from the rack, pulls at them and takes the whole thing out with him.

"Hey!" Charlie gets up. "Are you crazy?"

"WHERE IS HE?!"

WHOOSH!

Oops indeed.

Charlie's thrown at the wall like a rubber ball, only he doesn't bounce back. It feels like an invisible wrestler is keeping him in place, pinned by the throat. As if his head wasn't hurting enough.

When the force lets go and he drops to the floor, Charlie crawls on his butt to cower against the corner, his chest heaving uncontrollably, all while Henry steps forward.

"I'm gonna ask one more time."

*

"Ya shoulda seen it, I mean, I hit him *hard*, and he went down like –"

Francis holds up his index finger to shush Rick. His phone is vibrating. David calling.

"Hello?" my son answers, grinning expectantly.

On the other side, David feels his stomach doing a sailor's knot. "I have the key."

Francis paces around the front yard at Beresford Lot. "Atta boy. How'd you manage that?"

"Thomas is back. I snatched it without him noticing."

"Oh," Francis says, his smile dropping, "alright then." I can't tell if he's disappointed at how anti-climactic this answer is or worried that Thomas is back. Both?

"Where do we make the exchange?" David asks, his heart doing jumping-jacks.

Francis takes his sweet time to answer, as if to torture him. Then, "The Monastery Arena."

David gets a chill when the call is ended.

Back at Beresford, Rick himself is on pins and needles, his hands over the handle of a shovel stuck to the ground. "What he say? What he say?"

"We're a go. But there's a potential problem: Thomas is back in town. Won't be long till he catches on and tries to stop his Godfather." He points at Rick with the phone in his hand. "That's where you come in."

Rick nearly drools out the corner of his wicked mouth.

"'Bout damn time ya asked."

*

At the Ford apartment, back in the city, Walt's eye has started twitching, in response to the incessant banging coming from the door to his kids' room. Every knock on wood is a hammer pounding into his brain.

He finally snaps and trots down the hall, opening the door in a huff and shouting, "I swear to God, I am gonna wring –"

When Martin backs away from him with a shriek, Walt is stunned stupid. What the actual –?

His younger son shrugs his shoulders and lifts his palms.

"Abwacadabwa?"

*

"Are you feeling better?"

Nicole removes a wet cloth from her aunt's forehead. Celeste lay in her couch, eyes closed, recuperating from her earlier shock. Telling her life story in one fell swoop felt like having her insides pumped out, mushed up, and shoved back in. Her strength was slowly returning, but her migraine worsened by the minute. Still, she mustered a faint nod for her niece.

"Good," Nicole says, "now, Aunt Cel. Please forgive me, but there's something I have to ask you."

Rocky's woken up from his nap by the metal door pulling up. He jumps in a fright and growls, in anticipation of the intruder.

When he sees Nicole at the entrance to the bull pen, his baby blues sparkle like they never have before.

He squeals, he screeches, he utters every gleeful sound his muzzle will allow him to. Nicole crouches down and takes him in her arms, teary-eyed from the reunion.

"Oh, honey! It's okay, I'm here, I'm gonna get you out."

She examines the metal chain that Rocky's collar was swapped for, and the large lead ball it's attached to. "God, they really went all out," she says, wondering how she can get him free.

But all manner of thought leaves her head when the back of it is met by the barrel of a gun.

"Look at this now."

Nicole brings up her trembling hands and slowly gets back on her feet, while Rocky whimpers below. Behind her back, Francis strokes Nicole's hazel hair, whilst pressing the gun firmly against it.

"Never seen a girl bullfighter," he says. "Have you?"

*

Thomas and Alfie take a seat at the playground. Well, Alfie takes a seat – Thomas walks in circles before him, nearly making his friend dizzy.

"Grandpa must have found out she had an abortion," Thomas theorizes, "Miss Colm said they both had affairs, maybe he wasn't so forgiving either. She didn't want him to know she was carrying a love child, and when he found out at last, they got in an argument, and she killed him."

"You say your whole family's involved though," Alfie tells him, "would they have protected their mom if she killed, well, their dad?"

"Good question," Thomas concedes.

"Also, where does the money factor in? I thought that had something to do with it."

Thomas stops and puffs. "I am in way over my brilliant head."

"Read the letter again, maybe something will stand out to you this time."

Thomas figures he may as well. He reaches into this pocket for the printout and –

"Wait a minute."

"What?"

Thomas pulls out the inside of all his pocket. "The key! The key is gone!"

"What key?"

"I had the key to the treasure chest, the one Miss Colm talked about, and now it's –" He stops and frowns. "Godpa."

Without warning, Thomas flees the scene again.

Alfie shakes his head in disbelief. "Are you fricking kidding me?"

Thomas barges into David's house – he has a habit of doing that.

"Godpa! Godpa!"

As per usual, Alfie follows him in. "Thomas, what's going on?"

Thomas looks around the living room, even checking behind the door. "We have to find him; he's taken my key and God knows what he's gonna –"

When he turns around and sees what's coming out of the kitchen, he gasps and falls flat on his butt. Alfie steps back to keep from being hit by his friend. When he looks up, his eyes are caught in the shine of a blade.

Before the sink, Rick brandishes the meat cleaver he retrieved from the cutlery drawer. His grin bigger and more dangerous than the knife.

"Leavin' already?" the bully says, "Y'all just got here."

*

The walk to the arena feels like marching off to war. David's red flip-flops tap the pavement in a steady rhythm as the hot air rises all around him, making the road ahead look wavy. With every step he takes, the arena comes further into view, rising from the ground, all big, and round, and white. David can almost hear the soundtrack of some action movie's big climax playing in his head. Inside the ring, his uncle awaits him, like an executioner standing at the scaffold.

When David arrives, he's surprised to find someone there already. Staring blankly at the ring, arms at his sides.

"Henry?"

"I couldn't go in."

David approaches him. "What are you doing here?"

"Rocky's there." Moving just one finger, but not the rest of his hand, Henry points at the arena. "I came to get him, but – I couldn't go in."

David is stumped. "How did – why can't you?"

Henry's vacant expression morphs into a sad one. "I know there's trouble inside."

David breathes in, his own eyelids drooping. "Yep. Trouble."

"Why did we do all this?" Henry asks.

"What?"

"This Grandpa thing. Why did we have to know what happened to him?"

David pockets his hands. "I guess we were curious. Someone in the family did kill him, it's a bit scary. Didn't you want to know?"

Henry tilts his head slightly. "I guess. But now –"

"Yeah?"

Henry finally looks at him. "Now *everything* is scary. Everyone. My dad, and Grandma; Uncle Francis, even Thomas. Fred went away, Rocky's locked up, Nana will never move again, and Pop died. We made all of that happen."

David breathes in before saying something. "I guess we thought learning the truth was better than not knowing."

Henry looks back at the ring with pouted lips. "I liked not knowing."

David doesn't answer, but he realizes so did he. He looks up and imagines the arena coming to life and calling out his name; beckoning him to step forward with one hand, enticing and reassuring, yet the other hand behind its back, holding some kind of weapon.

But he still clutches the key in his pocket and walks on.

Time for the big climax.

***

Co-Starring
Alistair Palmer
Barnaby Arnold   *Clare Colm*   *Della Towers*
Ferdinand Plum   *Geoffrey Betts*   *Horace Towers*
Janice Penshaw   *Joanna Spyder*   *Oliver Doggo*
Penelope Colm   *Perry Lawson*   *Ray Carson*

Written & Directed by
Renato Belindro

Unanswered Questions

- Who killed Albert? Why?
- ~~Who was the letter addressed to?~~
- ~~What money is Albert referring to?~~
- ~~How does Francis know about the money?~~
- Why is Doris blackmailing Cassandra?
- ~~Where did the second letter come from? And the other letters?~~
- ~~Who is Francis' real mother?~~
- ~~Whose blood is on the crib?~~
- What is the significance of 77-04-09?
- ~~What is the key for?~~
- ~~What happened at Beresford Lot?~~
- Where did the bloodied toy car come from?
- Why does Cassandra owe Madam Witch?

Next time, on Monastery

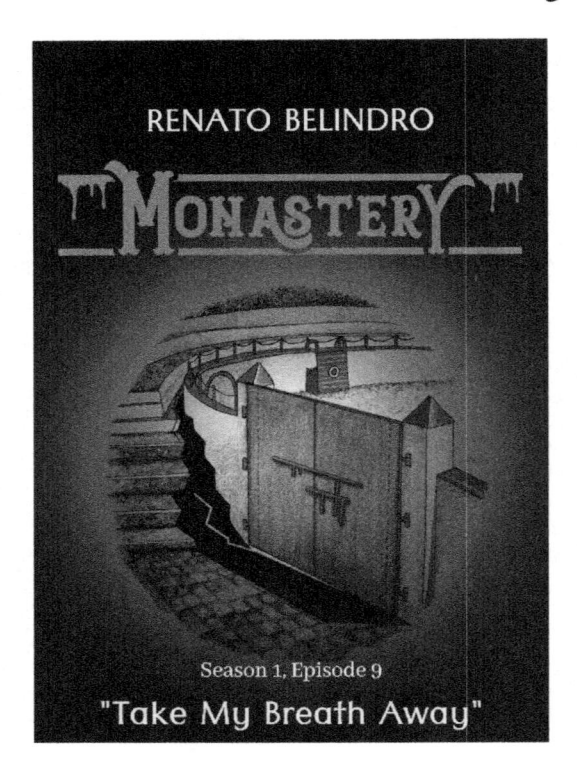

David and Thomas brace themselves for the conflict of their lives, when the former squares off with his vindictive uncle, and the latter is held hostage by the playground bully. Meanwhile, Monastery opens its doors to an intriguing new neighbor, and Albert opens his arms to welcome a loved one.

The Author

Renato Belindro hails from Portugal and studied Law at the University of Coimbra. He then moved to the UK to pursue his dream of writing. He has an MA in Creative Writing from Coventry University, where he was invited to lecture in novel planning and screenwriting, among other modules. His work tends to mix drama, comedy, and mystery. *Monastery*, which includes all three, is his debut novel.

Printed in Great Britain
by Amazon